THE LOST WORLD

HOUNDS ABROAD: BOOK ONE

Lily's life was dog-free and uneventful until one night when it became absolutely the reverse.

That same night Matt Lannings was reluctantly drawn into the fantastical scenario that Lily's life had become – the only thing was that Lily believed she'd been chosen to save another world in another universe – and Matt didn't.

Matt didn't believe any of it!

Susan Alison lives in Bristol, UK, and writes and paints full-time. She paints dogs, especially Border Collies, Corgis, Whippets and Greyhounds. Every now and then she paints something that is *not* a dog just to show she's not completely under the paw – mainly, she's under the paw…

Short stories of hers (*not* usually about dogs) have been published in women's magazines worldwide.

In 2011 she was presented with the Katie Fforde Bursary Award (with which she's incredibly chuffed).

She has a dog blog (with the occasional non-dog painting) at www.MontyandRosie.blogspot.com, and a website at www.SusanAlison.com, and if you'd like to receive her (very occasional) newsletter in the comfort of your own inbox, there is a space to put your email address on the bottom of any page on her website.

Also by Susan Alison and available now…

Romantic Comedies:

White Lies and Custard Creams
Romantic comedy with a dash of mystery.
#1 best-selling novel!!!

All His Own Hair
Romantic comedy with a dash of sabotage.

Out from Under the Polar Bear
Romantic comedy with a dash of manky polar bear.

KATIE FFORDE: *"Susan Alison handles difficult issues with quirky humour and uplifting results."*

JILL MANSELL: *"Susan Alison has written a lovely, quirky romp packed with off-the-wall characters - original, intriguing and great fun!"*

Illustrated Doggerel:

The Corgi Games
Welsh Corgi dogs engage in various forms of sport (including sack racing) in their usual stylish and winning way. In rhyme. Natch.

The illustrations throughout the paperback version of this book are in full colour.

Woofs of Wisdom on Writing
Woofs on Writing dictated to Susan by CorgiScribe, and illustrated in full colour throughout.

Sweet Peas and Dahlias (and other illustrated short stories): Very short, twisty stories about love in different guises

This is a petite volume of five stories just right for reading in a spare moment. Take a break - put your feet up - have a laugh, or an ahhhhhh, or a surprise at the twist in the tail of the tale!

The illustrations were especially commissioned from the talented, and sadly missed, Wendi Fyers to add another dimension to your reading pleasure.

* * * * *

See the author's artwork blog at www.MontyandRosie.blogspot.com for book news and paintings or go to www.SusanAlison.com and sign up to receive the news directly in to your inbox.

Susan Alison

The Lost World
Hounds Abroad: Book One

An Urban Fantasy

Copyright © 2015 Susan Alison

The right of Susan Alison to be identified as the Author of the Work has been asserted by her in accordance with the Copyright, Designs and Patents Act 1988.

First published in 2015 © Susan Alison

Apart from any use permitted under UK copyright law, this publication may only be reproduced, stored, or transmitted, in any way, shape or form, or by any means, with prior permission in writing of the author, or in the case of reprographic production, in accordance with the terms of the licences issued by the Copyright Licensing Agency.

All characters in this publication are fictitious,
and any resemblance to real persons, living or dead, is purely coincidental.

Except for Seb.

ISBN-13: 978-1497309470
ISBN-10: 1497309476

website and newsletter sign-up form: www.SusanAlison.com
dog blog: www.MontyandRosie.blogspot.com

ACKNOWLEDGEMENTS

My special thanks go to my son without whose constant encouragement no stories of mine would ever get on a page. He's simply the best!

The lovely Katie Fforde has done me proud with her fab words about my book – thank you so much!

I particularly want to thank Richard, Karen, Helen and Tracey for reading through my manuscript. Any mistakes found in this book will be down to me.

As always, I acknowledge that life would be generally flatter, greyer and so much more sweetly scented and boring, without my dogs.

Cover art by Susan Alison

For Richard

Simply the Best

Chapter One

Whoever was at her door was very impatient, although Lily didn't blame them for that – it was a filthy night. As she hurried from her study and down the hall, she could hear the rain hitting the ground with such force that she'd be surprised to find any earth left in her garden when the storm died down. The wind added to the chaos by moaning and howling. Who would be out on such a night? The very question made her pause – who *would* be out on such a night? And she didn't have a spy-hole in her door. She'd been meaning to get one installed for ages.

As though her visitor knew of her hesitation he thumped on her front door again. It was an imperious command as if to say she should stop being so sluggardly, and jump to obey. Lily hissed through her teeth. She disliked him already.

The banging on the door redoubled both in volume and in pace. Whoever was out there was shouting at her through his fists, pounding on the door as though to smash it in, sod waiting! The storm also increased in ferocity, its efforts at tearing down the close-knit houses in her street no doubt resulting in flying roof tiles capable of decapitating unwary passers-by.

Reaching the door, Lily hesitated. It *was* late, and she was on her own. Leaning against it, she shouted, "Who's there?"

But no matter how hard she pressed her head to the door she could hear nothing but the wind and the rain and the clatter of flying objects, and then she heard a yelp as though one of those missiles had connected with her visitor. Now without thinking she threw back the bolts, turned the key and pulled. It didn't take much effort because as soon as there was a gap the storm whirled in and slammed the door back against the wall, narrowly missing her. She leaned out into the night, but could see no one.

As well as a spy-hole, she needed to get the light on the front of her house fixed. She couldn't see anything even with the street lamp just down the road. In the murky night air its orange glow didn't spread very far. Puzzled, she looked all around, her hair flying across her face, slapping into her eyes. She made to step back into her house when she heard someone say: *Take me in. Take me in.*

The voice was very clear with an underlying current of anxiety. It made Lily feel desperate. The owner of that voice needed her, and with no idea of how she knew, she knew she needed him, too.

She felt compelled to look down. There had been a definite yelp of pain and she dreaded seeing a body, or an injured person, lying on her doorstep. But all she saw was a black mass, blacker than the night that surrounded it. From that mass the merest glint of light showed, disappeared and showed again repeatedly as though from an eye blinking against the force of the storm. She was being stared at in a way that made her feel there was nothing else in the universe to look at but her.

It was a dog! Or maybe a wolf. It appeared to be very large.

Take me in. Take me in.

"Oh my God!" Lily fell to her knees. "You poor thing." She held her hands out to the dog at the same time the thought flashed across her mind that it was probably a stupid thing to do. He might take a chunk out of her.

No, I won't.

"You might." Lily found herself saying out loud. By this time her hands were on his coat. To her distress she could feel bones even though his fur was very thick. He was also soaking wet.

It's bloody cold out here.

"Let's get you inside." She stood up and held the door open in the eternal welcoming gesture: do enter my home. She was amazed that this creature, totally unknown to her, could so immediately take up residence in her head. She had instantly felt such empathy with him, as if he'd been missing from her life without her realising, but now he was here she was complete.

"Stop being fanciful, Lily!" she muttered.

She'd never had a dog, not as a child, and not since leaving home either. It was something she'd thought about. Constantly. But she was afraid of getting too attached, and then she'd lose it, and then it would be awful. Given the number of rescue dogs that desperately needed homes she felt guilty about this, but still, she was afraid.

That's very cowardly of you, if you don't mind my saying so.

"Don't start that," Lily whispered. "I feel bad enough as it is. I'm not going through all the arguments again." Weariness overcame her just thinking about it, let alone indulging in the circular bickering with herself that never stopped.

This night's unexpected visitor went ahead of her, and with more help from the storm than she wanted, Lily slammed the door, making its frame shudder. The wind seemed to howl even more loudly in frustration at being shut out. Something made her pause and turn the key in the deadlock too, although usually she was a bit casual about security.

Bit too casual if you ask me.

"I didn't," she murmured taking the keys from the door and placing them on the bookshelf in the hall so that whoever was out there trying to get in couldn't somehow get hold of the keys if she left them in the door. She'd seen too many films where doing so led to disaster. She didn't feel so bad talking to herself now she had a dog here. She could pretend she was talking to him. What was more natural than talking to your dog?

Feeding him.

"Let's get you something to eat, Dog. Need to find you a name, don't we?"

They padded out to the kitchen and Lily inspected the contents of her fridge. "Hmm… nothing too exciting in here," she said gazing at a bag of limp celery, some mouldy cheese and a small tub of double cream she'd got to make chocolate sauce but hadn't bothered in the end. Dog shoved his head between her and the door frame and inspected the fridge himself.

No, you're right. Got anything in a tin instead? Corned beef? Tuna? Sausages?

Dog sat down and stared at her hopefully.

"What a good idea!" Lily opened the cupboard and pulled out a tin of corned beef, ripped off the opening key, and wound the strip back. Drool hung from Dog's mouth. Poor thing. He must be starving. Apparently, he was – he didn't even wait for the meat to hit the floor, but jumped up and snatched it from her hands before it was fully out of its tin. He made short work of it and spat the tin out.

"Don't ever do that again!" Lily scolded. "You can get a really nasty cut from a corned beef tin." She showed him the old white scar that crossed her hand but he merely looked at her hopefully again. "Surely you'll be sick if you've been starved and then suddenly have loads to eat," she said, looking back in the cupboard, nevertheless. "Maybe if you had some carbohydrate to mix in with the meat that would help." She pulled out an old bag of oats and made some porridge in the microwave, mixing in some maple syrup and cream to cool it down. He lapped it up, his tail waving gently from side to side like a heavy flag in a lazy wind.

Then he walked upstairs as though he'd been doing it all his life, threw himself with a huge sigh onto the big basket of clean washing she'd just neatly folded prior to putting away, and was instantly asleep, or so it seemed. Despite overflowing the basket on all sides, he was so completely relaxed that Lily, watching him, felt the call of slumber weigh her own eyelids down, and throwing her clothes off, she collapsed onto her bed. As she slid into a welcoming drowsiness she wondered how he'd managed to bang on her door in the first place. He'd made such a racket – how could he possibly have done that with just his paws? She also wondered what to call him.

Just call me Sam.

Okay.

Chapter Two

Three streets away from where Lily and Sam slept despite the escalating storm, Matt sank into his leather buttoned armchair and inhaled the scents from his malt whisky. The gale sounded like a living thing out there and he was grateful to be inside and off duty, not even on-call. He could feel himself relaxing, which was more than could be said for Amber. He'd never seen her so edgy; it must be the wind unsettling her. She'd been continuously on the move for the last couple of hours, almost creeping along the floor, her nose twitching, ears upright. An extra strong gust of wind and she'd leap up, all the fur along her back vertical. It was enough to spook Matt if he was that way inclined, just watching her. Luckily he wasn't that way inclined. Something he couldn't see wasn't going to spook him.

He held his hand out to her and she stopped pacing. Ears lowered, she crept over to him and leaned her chin on his knee, gazing up at him with her lovely, tawny eyes. He could feel the tension in her through that contact and he wondered again what had happened to this dog before she came into his life to make her so extraordinarily tense all the time.

Outside, something smacked into his front door and Amber was no longer on the floor, but trembling in a heap on his lap, her nose in his armpit. Carefully, he put the cut crystal tumbler on the coffee table and instead of turfing her off he closed his arms around her and hugged her close. Poor dog. She was in such a distressed state he couldn't stick to his rule about her not being a lap dog even though she was way too big and bits of her overflowed him.

At times like this he could swear she was trying to tell him something, but rationally he knew it was that his guard was down. Ever since Diane's desertion of him, and subsequent disappearance, he'd been much more fanciful about people and things communicating with him. This included house plants, inkjet printers and his car. Especially his car, which switched itself off just whenever it felt like it for no discernible reason the garage could find.

He knew that soon he had to pull himself together and face the world scientifically again, but if in the meantime a dog could give him any clues as to why, so near their wedding day, Diane had buggered off and left him, he'd be a lot better off than he was now, groping in the dark, having no clue as to what he'd done wrong.

If he never found out what he'd done wrong, it surely meant he'd go through a lifetime of doing it wrong again and again. Not that he had any intention of doing that – he was never asking for *that* trouble again! Bloody women! He snorted and Amber quivered harder.

"It's all right, girl," he murmured, stroking her fur, marvelling again at the silkiness of it. It was so much finer than any dog fur he'd come across before. "It's not you I'm being contemptuous about. It's me. As usual, I'm being far too fanciful for my own good. But, really, Diane would have loved you. She would. Maybe if you'd been around then, she wouldn't have left me."

To his surprise, he realised Amber was no longer shuddering. She was gazing unwaveringly at him and if he didn't know better he could swear compassion shone from her eyes. Her tongue shot out and lightly flicked the end of his nose as though he'd been kissed. His eyes instantly smarted with unshed tears and he hugged her even more tightly. He was so totally losing it! He'd better pull himself together soon or he'd be carted off and locked up, and who would look after Amber then?

An extra loud shriek from the wind and Amber leapt from his lap and transformed into a creature ready for a fight to the death. Matt watched in amazement. She looked twice her normal size, even her paws looked bigger. She stared at the sitting room door, her eyes flat and emotionless, her whole body ready for action; her teeth, which seemed longer and sharper were bared and glistening in a silent snarl.

Matt reached out to her but before he could say anything the door flew open and without hesitation Amber sprang forward. A growl so full of hate filled the room that Matt stopped where he was, shocked breathless. There **was** something there! There really was! It hadn't just been his lovely, over-sensitive Amber jumping and flinching at imaginings. He couldn't see it, but he could feel a malevolence so intensely alive that his skin felt as though it were peeling off of its own volition, trying to get away.

And yet, this was ridiculous! He was behaving like a spooked child at Halloween. Matt ran from the room after Amber only to see his front door wide open whipping back and forth in the tempest, banging off the wall, smashing off the frame, back and forth. There was no sign of Amber.

Had she gone outside? Into this weather? How had the door opened? What had happened to the evil presence he'd felt? He no longer sensed it and its occurrence had been so fleeting he now doubted himself. At the same time he was sure he could smell where it had been as though something actively decaying had lain there for decades.

But where was Amber? He couldn't bear to think of her out in this, alone and afraid. He grabbed his jacket and hurried out, only remembering to go back and shut his front door when he'd reached the garden gate. He was definitely losing it, coming unhinged since Diane's unexplained and inexplicable disappearance. And now he was being silly about what was nothing but a dog's neuroses. He should know better, but he couldn't help himself. The anxiety over Amber was all-pervasive and he knew he wouldn't rest until he was sure she was safe. He couldn't keep his fiancée safe, but he should be able to keep a dog safe, for Pete's sake!

He set off down the street even though it seemed impossible to track down a dog on a night like this. It was dark and confusing with so much movement all around him, and a lot of noise. How could he possibly find a dog if she didn't want to be found? But he couldn't just let her slide though his fingers like Diane had.

No matter what he suggested they try, nothing altered Diane's decision to leave him. How could she just give up on their relationship like that? Well, at least without discussing it with him. If that was indeed what she'd wanted he wouldn't have stood in her way. He believed everyone's life was their own to use as they saw fit, but she didn't even talk to him about it – as though any contribution he might make to a discussion was irrelevant. And to disappear... No one had thought anyone else was involved. Not even the police. No. It was all down to him, and her not wanting to be with him any more.

No matter how hard he tried, he couldn't shake off the conviction that somehow he should have been able to get through to her, but he'd never been able to find the words and he'd failed.

He plunged on through the night, his hands in his pockets, head pulled down into the collar of his entirely inadequate jacket.

Diane's parents also felt bad. Her mother was so confused. "But I brought her up to face everything, not run away. Why did she have to run away?" Her face would be a caricature of pained perplexity as she addressed Matt. The unspoken accusation was clear: "Why didn't she want to stay with you, Matt? What did you do to her that she didn't want to stay?" It was like a rusty screwdriver gradually being pushed through his heart again and again.

Something rushed at him out of the darkness and he ducked. Whatever it was flew by and crashed into someone's garden wall. If that had hit him he'd have been in trouble! He carried on, taking more care, but still couldn't get his mind off Diane.

Her father, always inarticulate, had patted him heavy-handedly on the shoulder and grunted something unintelligible. Diane's sister hadn't spoken to him since, and her brother had actually taken a swing at him. Luckily he'd been so drunk at the time that Matt had merely stepped back out of harm's way, and he'd fallen over. The embarrassment of the incident, however, had fuelled Keith's hatred of him and now Matt had a whole family of people he'd been fond of, and he thought fond of him, who hated him. He didn't need it. His contempt for himself made it quite unnecessary for anyone else to hate him, but he supposed they didn't know that.

He was just wandering aimlessly, now. There was no logical place to go, except home. But he didn't want to go back to that house without Amber. He ought to sell it, start afresh somewhere else, but he'd been hanging onto it as though Diane might appear at his door one day and things would go back to the way they'd been. He trudged on.

Chapter Three

Lily woke suddenly and lay, heart pounding heavily, trying to orient herself, trying to understand the tug in her mind. The strong smell of dog gave her a clue and she leapt out of bed. Sam was no longer in the washing basket. Lily pulled on jeans and boots and ran downstairs to find him staring at the front door. Automatically, as though programmed, she grabbed her jacket and wrestled the door open. He lunged out into the night. Without hesitation she locked the house and ran after him, almost immediately losing him in the dark. Now what?

She hesitated for a moment, but a strong sense of unease made her set off in pursuit. She hoped she was going in the right direction…

To avoid a man barging his way past, muttering to himself as he went, Lily had to quickly sidestep and nearly fell. A flying wheelie bin narrowly missed her. In dodging it she lost her footing and fell to the ground, scraping the palm of her hand quite badly. That was going to be sore when she got the feeling back! She hauled herself upright and struggled on. She didn't know where she was going, but the compulsion to go there was too strong to be questioned. Somehow Sam needed her. She knew it.

Around the next corner she spotted a maelstrom of ferocity. A blackness more dense than the night moved at such speed she couldn't really see it; flashes of light punctuated it at rapid intervals. But then, she noticed a lighter patch diving in and being thrown out only to dive in again.

And weaving between the two was a dank greyness hard to look at and impossible to describe. Lily ran towards it at the same time as cursing herself for being so stupid. Heaven knew what she was getting herself into. She ran anyway, but before she got there it was all over. The greyness disappeared on the wind with a long, wavering howl. And on the ground lay two dogs, shredded, bleeding and exhausted, surely mortally wounded.

"No!" she screamed and raced towards them. She noticed another figure running from the other direction and ran even harder in case whatever it was that had hurt them so badly was coming back to finish them off, if they weren't already done for. But she realised it was only a man. Even so, she reached the dogs and crouched protectively over them, despairing to see such awful wounds. She couldn't really see them on Sam, him being black and the night being dark, but the way he lay there so limp and exhausted told her the worst and his presence in her mind seemed dimmed. But she could see them on the other dog because of the lighter fur. Lily placed her palm on Sam's head and felt a quiver. He was still alive then. She held her hand out to the other dog and was shocked to have it knocked sharply aside by the man who had arrived and was now stooping over the dogs on the ground.

"Get away!" he shouted. "What have you done? Look at her. Your dog's killed her!"

He gathered the other dog up into his arms, his face so bleak and fierce, Lily's heart turned inside out in despair; his grief was so palpable, it was like a cheese grater across her knuckles. He turned away with the bundle clasped tenderly to his chest as though the dog was made of the most fragile glass lacework.

Lily stepped towards him. "Wait. Where are you going? She needs attention. We must try to do something."

"She'll get attention," he snapped. "I'm a vet. Think yourself lucky I'm not a policeman or I'd arrest you for having an uncontrollable animal that goes round killing other people's dogs. Now piss off!" He marched away.

"But there was something else there…" Realising she was wasting time, Lily looked back at Sam on the ground and noticed a little flicker of movement from his tail. He needed attention too! She knelt down and pushed her hands under him, braced herself and slowly stood erect, her knees feeling as though they would disintegrate with the effort.

I'm too heavy.

"I'll be the judge of that," she snarled, gritting her teeth, forcing her feet to get on with the job of putting one forward and following it with the other. She pursued the man, regardless that her heart was about to burst with the strain. Her dog needed a vet. That rude git was a vet. He was stuck with her and her dog whether he liked it or not. If he really was a vet he couldn't refuse to attend an animal in need of his skills. Could he?

She slogged after him, her legs buckling, her arms threatening to tear away from her body. After a while, which felt like a few hours, Sam lifted his head with some effort and leaned it on her shoulder. She had the unsettling feeling he was watching her now, up close and personal, but also a new strength ran through her and she got her second wind. Either that or the dog had miraculously lost half his bodyweight since she picked him up. No, it must be that she had reserves she hadn't realised she had in time of need. She took a firmer grip on Sam and hastened her steps so as not to lose Rude Git in the dark and confusion of the night, which although calmer now, was still an uncomfortable place to be.

As she walked, she grew stronger and stronger and Sam grew lighter and lighter and Lily felt more and more sure that she'd done the right thing in opening her door earlier that day and letting him in, scruffy mongrel though he looked. Was that a growl? Nah. She needed to get control of her imagination!

Arriving at the house into which Rude Git had disappeared, Lily found the door open. He must have been in too much of a hurry to close it, or maybe he'd been unable to because of carrying the dog. It was a relief to find she didn't have to break it down. Lily stepped into the hallway and pushed the door shut with her foot. She followed the light at the end of the hall, through a big kitchen and out into what looked like a vet's surgery behind it.

Relieved, she placed Sam on a table and stood back, expecting to find herself aching from the unaccustomed weight, but she seemed fine. She'd probably suffer in the morning.

Rude Git's dog lay on the other table. Lily was afraid to look in case the dog was dead. It had such dreadful injuries. How could it have survived? But when she made herself glance in that direction she saw the dog was sitting up gently licking Rude Git's arm. His hand was at his forehead, shading his eyes as though he had difficulty seeing in a glare of light. He was shaking his head and muttering: "How can this be?"

Lily approached the table and looked down the length of the dog's body. She could see nothing apart from shining, healthy, caramel-coloured fur, white on the legs and face and end of the tail. She could see no blood, no injuries, nothing. What on Earth? It made no sense.

She went back to Sam and ran her hands over him, parting his strong-black-coffee-coloured fur to see intact skin beneath. She could see nothing untoward.

"I didn't imagine it," she said. "I know I didn't. They'd been in a fight and they were injured. Both of them." She turned to Rude Git. "And they had **not** been in a fight with each other," she said loudly as though he was dim and any speech directed his way needed amplification. "They'd been in a fight with something else. They were both fighting something else."

But the look he gave her wasn't at all conciliatory. "They can't have been injured," he said slowly and very patiently. He was obviously using monumental restraint to be patient with this complete idiot who stood before him jabbering nonsense.

"*You* thought they'd been injured. That's why you were so vile about my dog. Now you're saying you didn't think they'd been injured, after all?"

"Well, look at them," he said sweeping his hand between the two dogs. Startled, Lily stepped back. She hadn't noticed Sam jump off the table. He was now sitting beside the other table, his nose a fraction away from the caramel and cream dog. "Do they look injured? Do they look bathed in blood and gore?"

"No," she admitted. "Not now they don't. But they were."

"Don't be ridiculous! They can't have been!"

"But they were."

"They can't have been."

"But they were."

He merely stared at her, frustration and scorn clear in his eyes.

"Well," Lily said. "I don't know how they were and now they're not, but I refuse to doubt myself to that extent. There must be another answer."

"Like what?" He leaned back against the wall, crossed his arms, and put on a face of feigned interest, waiting for an explanation he would clearly argue with the second it left her lips.

Lily flattened her irritation and made her voice level. "Um. Well. They could be a particular breed of dog that heals at an astonishing rate."

"I'm a vet. I've never come across such a thing."

"Just because *you've* never heard of it, doesn't mean it can't exist," she said sharply. Honestly. The ego on him…

But she wasn't going to mention the strength she'd found to carry Sam. Looking at him now she had no idea how she'd managed it. Having said that, she had heard stories of women able to lift cars up when their children had been trapped underneath, and other superhuman feats of strength when loved ones were in danger. No, she wasn't going to tell Rude Git that. It did sound a bit far-fetched, and she'd only known Sam a few hours – it wasn't as if he could possibly come into the 'loved ones' category. Not to mention being a dog…

Oy! Loved one. I can be too. As for 'just a dog' - you should be ashamed of yourself, young pup!

Eek! Lily managed to stop herself apologising to Sam, but only just, and only because of the company she was in.

Rude Git regarded her for a moment and said. "I think you'd better go home. And take that animal with you." He gestured towards Sam with his head and was greeted with a lifted lip and the sight of a magnificent set of fangs. Lily was surprised to see a cream paw shoot out from the auburn bundle of fur and smack Sam on the nose. He immediately bowed his head and looked as though he'd been really, really told off. He peered up at the other dog, his look of repentance so exaggerated Lily nearly laughed.

"We're very happy to go home," Lily said and marched to the door, but when she looked back it was to see Sam still sitting where he'd been and looking like he had no intention of leaving. She could have cried. Sam was her dog and he was abandoning her to stay here with Rude Git. It didn't matter that they'd only known each other a few hours. She'd thought they had a bond.

What? 'Just a dog', *not a loved one? A bond?*

She stared at him mutely, willing him to follow her voluntarily but he didn't budge. "Oh, all right – I'm sorry," she said, not looking at Rude Git. "Can we go now?" She waved her hand at Sam in a beckoning gesture. In doing so, she caught sight of her palm. "Ooh, look! Blood!" she shrieked triumphantly. "Look, Rude G… er, person – blood!" she waved her hand at him.

Clever girl. You've got him now.

She glanced at Sam. He thumped his tail encouragingly. She'd been forgiven.

"See," she said to Rude Git. "There's blood on my hands. From the dog. From Sam. What about your hands? You will have got blood from Caramel Girl, too. I have no explanation for why the dogs no longer have blood on them, but here is proof that there **was** blood on them." And she flapped her hand about some more as he stood there, arms folded, an air of waiting about him.

"Well?" she demanded impatiently.

He merely held his hands up to her. They were clean.

"But you will have washed them before you saw to Caramel Girl, won't you? I hope."

"Of course!"

"Do you remember if there was blood on them?"

"No, I don't remember. It's not Caramel Girl. It's Amber. And obviously there was no blood on them because there were no wounds to get the blood from."

He's gonna be a hard bone to crack, this one.

Rude Git approached, grabbed her hand, stared at it, and dragged her to the sink. "For Pete's sake! Look at the state of your hand. That's where the blood's come from. And it needs cleaning." And he proceeded to do just that regardless of Lily's protests.

"Ow. Ow. Ow." What the hell was he putting on it? It felt like a thousand flesh-eating ants had got into it.

"You must have fallen and put your hand out to save yourself. This will be sore for a few days, but at least it's clean now." And he tossed it back to her as though the feel of it was distasteful. "You can go home now. And take him with you," he said, waving in Sam's direction.

"He doesn't want to come with me," Lily said.

"I don't care. You're not leaving that biscuit bag here!" Rude Git insisted.

Not biscuit bag. Sausage bag. Mmm... sausagesss...

Lily didn't know what to do. She didn't actually **want** to leave that biscuit bag here, but if he didn't want to go with her, she couldn't see that it was within her power to do anything about it. Irresolute, she stood in the doorway ostentatiously ignoring Rude Git. But then she noticed Caramel Girl nudge Sam as though she'd said something to him and was insisting on it. Sam got up and lolloped over to Lily. He stuck his nose in her not-sore hand and then left the room.

Come on.

Lily did as she was bid and slunk out after him into the night, which by this time had completely calmed down as though washed clean of all fury.

At home again, with Sam ensconced in the washing basket, this time lined with an old duvet, and Lily in her own bed propped up against the headboard, she wondered if any of it had actually happened. The only thing she knew for certain was that a large, black and incredibly hairy dog-wolf-creature had turned up on her doorstep and seemed to be staying.

Lily smiled. She could live with that.

As for Rude Git, it was not as if she'd ever have to see him again, so all was right with her world, then.

Switching off the light, blissful sleep enfolded her more completely and seamlessly than it had in years.

Chapter Four

The morning dawned bright and lucid with a pale lemon wash across the sky. The smell of clean laundry had momentarily taken over from the smell of dirty bus exhaust and the usual not-so-fresh smells associated with a big city. Lily felt well, very well. She couldn't remember the last time she'd consciously felt as well as she did now.

She jumped out of bed and fell over a pile of black fur lying on the floor. Lily twisted in mid-air to avoid splitting her head open on the dressing table. Landing on the carpet she lay there and inspected the dog-wolf. His eyes were open, at once innocent and full of ancient knowledge, and laughing at her. She crawled over to him and started to part his fur systematically over his body. It was certainly very puzzling. There were no marks on him. She was so sure that he'd been mangled to death last night. Maybe she **was** losing it.

Nah, you're not losing it. I **was** *wounded. Horribly wounded. Wounded near to death. But we're special creatures, us Hounds of the Realm. We heal very quickly, miraculously quickly; even, one might say, supernaturally quickly. Especially while we're in the Human Territories. We've been given the power for this visit. So you did see what you thought you saw. It's just that we healed up.*

The voice was so clear in her head that she swivelled around to see if someone had entered the room behind her.

Nah. It's me. You're hearing me. You've been hearing me all along. But like most humans you choose to ignore the evidence of your own senses.

Carefully, Lily turned back to Sam to take another look.

Seb! It's Seb. Short for Sebastian. Meaning revered or majestic. Not Sam! That would make me a Samson, meaning sun-child or bright sun. Phooey. Just look at me. Do I look like a creature of the sun? That unreliable disc in the sky that allows clouds to put it out whenever they feel like it. Not on your bones I do!*

He sounded quite peeved.

She could have sworn she'd 'heard' Sam the previous night.

Nah! Sebbbbb...

Seb, she thought hurriedly. Seb. She put her hand out towards him, but before it met his fur, she lowered it to the floor to make sure she really was here. She patted and thumped the floor a few times until she hurt her fist. It certainly felt as though she was really here.

For the love of bones!!! You are hearing me speak to you!

He sounded impatient now. A little spark of fear blossomed. This dog was rather large and fierce and he was impatient with her. Lily drew back. He stared at her and suddenly showed all his teeth. The effect was so startlingly awful that she squeaked, leapt back and smacked into the dressing table. That particular item of furniture was always trying to get her. Now it had succeeded. Stunned, she lay on the carpet wondering if she was about to be savaged and left for dead.

I was smiling! Didn't you like my smile? I was smiling to make you feel comfortable. What more do you want me to do? Tell you a joke?

She rubbed hard at the back of her head, certain she could feel a lump growing under her hand. A lump the size of a duck egg. Not that she'd ever seen a duck's egg… "Tell me a joke, then!" she said grumpily.

Then she realised she'd spoken aloud. Not only spoken aloud to a dog but demanded he tell her a joke…

There, see. You can do it. Good girl. He showed her his teeth again.

She gave in entirely. She might as well just go along with it, humour him, give in to her obvious concussion. "You were smiling?" she asked. "That was a smile? Do it again."

Obediently, Seb showed her his teeth again. It was certainly an imposing array of glistening fangry, an arsenal of serious weaponry.

Not bad, ay? I've always looked after them, mind.

"What about this joke, then?"

Um. Did you hear the one about the zoo with only one dog in it?

"No. What about the zoo with only one dog in it?"

It was a shit zoo.

"I don't get it," Lily said. "A shit zoo... Oh – hang on – a Shih Tzu. Oh!" Lily fell about laughing so hard she rolled back into the dressing table again.

Uh, it's not that funny. It's just the only one I know. I normally rely on my natural wit, charm and intelligence rather than jokes as such.

Lily stopped laughing instantly. "No, none of this is that funny if it means I'm going to be carted off by the men in white coats. Who'll look after you then?"

It's not me that needs looking after. I'm here to look after you.

"You're not doing a very good job of it are you? All you've done so far is get me involved in fights in the night, make some complete stranger be really rude to me and then drive me out of my mind and it's only a matter of time before you get me locked up by the men in white coats."

*Who **are** these men?* Seb sat up, all alert, head whipping from side to side.

"It's just an expression. It means I've gone doolally and been taken away and locked up."

Doolally?

"That's a slang word for becoming unbalanced, losing my mental competence."

Look, stick to English, could you. That's bad enough, without some other language thrown in as well. Either that or you'll have to learn Hound. Mind you, doolally is a good word. I like it.

"Okay. Whatever you say."

Good girl. Now it's breakfast time. What've you got?

21

"Uh. I usually have a piece of toast."

Seb, his ears flattened to his head, gave her such an incredulous stare that Lily found herself gabbling, "But I have a fancy for egg and bacon this morning. I'll just rush out and get some…" The relief she felt when his face returned to some semblance of dogginess was so intense that she nearly fell over again.

Dressed and about to leave the house, she found Seb by her side. "You can't come," she said. "Dogs aren't allowed in shops." She turned away muttering, "I can't believe I'm talking to this dog."

I'm coming with you. Just get the door open. You can't be allowed out on your own. I have to look after you.

"I've looked after myself perfectly well for years," she snapped.

Yes, and just look at the job you've made of it. Are you happy? No. Is your fur shiny? No. Are all your teeth complete and sharp? Nope – you have a mass of metal in the back one on the left. Have you someone who hunts for you and protects you? Nope. Have you someone into whose warmth you fold yourself on cold nights? Nope. Have you a litter of puppies hidden somewhere that I can't see? Nope. Didn't think so.

"Thank you, but I don't see having puppies as the be-all and end-all of my life's purpose! I am perfectly happy!" Lily stomped off down the path.

I think you should lock the door.

She stomped back up the path and locked the door. He was infuriating!

Lily strode ahead but Seb kept pace with her whilst expending no effort at all; Lily ended up gasping for breath until giving it up as a bad job and adopting her normal walking pace.

Good girl.

When they reached the local store, Lily walked in without a backward glance, snatched up a basket and rushed around the shelves. Seb stayed outside as though he knew he wasn't allowed in. She threw bacon in her basket, and sausages – at which point she could have sworn an approving: '*Food of the Dogs*!' roared through her head, so she threw in another packet and was rewarded with an even greater blast of approval. Black pudding, eggs, kidneys, bread and butter. She paid and left the shop to find Seb sitting outside next to the post put there for the purpose of tying your dog to it, ignoring a group of youths who were jumping at him and then away as though they were tempting him to lunge for them.

"Oy! Stop teasing him," she shouted. Ignorant oiks. What was the matter with people?

The oiks transferred their attention to her instead, and crowded in too close…

Seb casually got to his paws, padded to her side, and smiled widely at his would-be tormentors. Transfixed by the sight of his smile, they froze in place until he moved even closer. They ran screaming.

Heck heck. They thought I was tied up. Heck, heck.

Seb's nose was down by his paws, his shoulders shook and Lily, initially worried he was choking, realised he was laughing.

They thought I was tied to the post. Heck heck heck.

"Yeah. They did," she chortled, but not for long. Sometimes she despaired of the human race. The oiks had only been provoking him because they thought he couldn't answer them back. One of them even had the nerve to shout over his shoulder, as he ran off: "Oy, missus. You're supposed to tie your dog up. He could have bitten us."

They were only puppies.

"They weren't only puppies! And so what, even if they were!" she said, opening the gate to the front garden and frightening the postman who'd just been pushing something through her letter box. He leapt back and stumbled over his bag, but managed to catch himself before he fell.

"Oh, sorry. It's just me. I've started talking to myself," she mumbled.

"That's okay. Sometimes it's the only way to get any intelligent conversation," he said, rushing off without quite looking at her.

Why didn't you tell him you were talking to me?

She gave Seb a searing look. But she'd obviously have to practice her searing looks as he simply gazed back at her, an enquiring angle to his ears – the very picture of intense puzzlement.

"Let's get breakfast," she said, resignation settling on her heart. Maybe a good breakfast would put her right. Seb galloped off down the hallway and was sitting expectantly in the kitchen when she got there.

"What did you mean you were here to look after me?" she queried as she poked at the sausages. She tended to overcook sausages. She didn't like them – heaven knew what went into them, but she'd thought a dog might like them.

Food of the Dogs!

She was still going to cook them to death just in case, not wanting to give him food poisoning even if he was a very annoying dog.

How very thoughtful of you.

"The postman was right. Talking to yourself **is** the only way to get any sensible conversation."

Heck, heck.

It must just be the late and unsettled night that had done it. Probably she would get through today, get a good night's sleep tonight and tomorrow she'd be back to normal.

You're normal already. You can hear me speak to you. Now stop doubting yourself. We're never going to be able to get stuff done if you insist on disbelieving your own senses. Honestly, you humans!

Seb shook his head like he was tried beyond all enduring, but yet he marvelled at his own patience. Or at least, Lily read his head-shaking like that. He might just have an itch inside his ear for all she knew.

Heck! Anyway, to get back to your question – I'm here to look after you because you're in danger. I'm also here because we're in danger, too, and somehow you help save us. So I must keep you safe from the danger so that you can save us from the other danger. I don't know if you're in danger because of being the reason we're saved, but whatever it is, that's why I'm here.

"Oh, I see," she said, not seeing much at all. "So, you're not here for me. You're here for you."

Well, of course. It's the same thing.

She stared at him. Well, of course.

The sausages are burnt enough now and the eggs are hard and the bacon's crisp and the black pudding is difficult to tell, but I expect it's cooked enough now. Come on, I'm starving!

It seemed rude to go and eat at her dining table and leave Seb eating from a bowl on the floor in the kitchen, and there was no way she was going to have him eating at the table, whether he was a talking dog or not.

Not exactly talking...

So she perched on a stool and ate her breakfast from the side in the kitchen while he wolfed his down from a rather nice bowl her mother had given her as a new home present when she moved in here. Her mother would be snitty as all hell if she knew her present was being used as a dog's breakfast bowl.

That's why you served my breakfast in it, isn't it.

"Yes," she giggled.

Heck, heck. Are we going round to see your dam and sire today?

Yes, but how did you know?

Ah ha! There's no end to my knowledge, my mysterious ways, and supernatural powers.

"You read my diary," she stated flatly, as though that was exactly what she'd expect a nosy dog to do. After all, if she could imagine a dog talking to her, she could imagine a dog reading her diary, too.

Yeah. Well, you left it open. We're a naturally curious lot. What is life without curiosity after all? By the way, that wasn't a bad breakfast. Not bad at all. Thank you very much!

He promptly fell full length on the floor and commenced snoring.

"You're welcome," she muttered, wiping the brown sauce from her plate with her last bite of toast. Piling the washing up in the sink she went off to get ready and with sinking heart realised that the unaccustomed breakfast feast had made her late. This wasn't going to go down well with her parents. Nor was a dog… Maybe she could sneak off while he was asleep and go alone. She wouldn't be that long. She was only delivering a box of cards. Seb might not even notice. She grabbed her jacket and the box and sidled down the hall towards the front door.

Oy! Wait for me. Seb came galloping out of the kitchen. She heard him, and the house felt him, before she saw him. The floor seemed to bounce with the vibration of his passing.

You don't want to leave me behind. I'll help you see things differently. I will.

"What do you mean?"

It's obvious you're reluctant to go round to your old den. You're probably misreading things. Humans always do. I can help you see stuff you haven't seen before. It's part of my job, too.

"Thanks for that. I'm sure that'll be very helpful," she said. "They don't even like dogs."

Luckily, I'm no ordinary dog am I? They'll love me. Don't worry.

How could a dog look smug? Can dogs look smug? This one looked smug, she was sure of it.

Yep. This is me looking smug. Just so you know.

Right. She wasn't going to think anything else. Nothing was safe to be thought around this dog. Even while she was thinking this she knew she was in serious trouble. Had she actually suffered a concussion? Was she really ill but didn't realise it yet?

Nope. You're fine. You're just a bit slow on the uptake, that's all. When you accept that we can communicate with each other life will get a lot easier and we can get on and do stuff.

"What stuff?"

The stuff I've come here to do, apart from looking after you. We have the Realm to save.

The Realm? She wasn't going to ask. No way was she going to ask. She scrunched her brain down on itself in an attempt to keep her thoughts mute.

Heck, heck, heck.

Outside, she locked up her house, unlocked her car, went round to the boot and lifted the lid, pleased she happened to own an estate car so Seb could get in the back bit.

I'm not getting in there. He leapt in though, but promptly slithered over the back seat and then into the front passenger seat.

Lily shouted at him through the boot, "You're not sitting in the front! It's dangerous. Get back here! If I have to stop suddenly or someone hits us, you should be okay in here." She waited. Nothing happened. "Seb! Get back here!"

Nothing happened.

"Seb!" she yelled.

A passer-by stopped and said, "That's no way to talk to your dog. If you sound angry with him why on Earth should he come to you?"

"Because he knows perfectly well what he's doing," Lily snapped. She was cross, but didn't have the nerve to tell the busybody to mind her own business.

"Don't be silly," Busybody said. "He's a dog. He can only take his cues from you." The admonishment was accompanied by a withering look. Lily felt a couple of centimetres high.

Shout at me again. Go on, sound angry. Shout again.

She didn't hesitate. It was exactly what she wanted to do anyway. "Seb!" she screamed. "Get your furry black butt back here this minute!"

"There's no way on Earth that dog is going to..." Busybody started. And then stopped.

Seb crawled over into the back seat and then slithered like thick black liquid into the boot. His ears flat to his head and with his nose down submissively, he crawled over to Lily and licked her hand. Once. At the same time he looked up at her so that white shone around the bottom of his pupils like crescent moons. He was the picture of abject shame and embarrassment. He was so very, very sorry for misbehaving.

Don't laugh!

Lily struggled with herself but managed to keep her face straight. "I'm sorry," she said to Busybody. "You were saying?"

Busybody snorted in an unladylike manner, muttered something about bullies, and marched off.

Lily stood there for a moment staring at Seb, then she bent over until she was nose-to-nose with him. "We really *are* communicating aren't we? I'm not insane am I? We can actually speak to each other, although speaking isn't really the right term. It's true isn't it?"

Yep!

Lily and Seb straightened up at the same time so their heads were still on a level, as though their eyes were joined. "I can't tell you how privileged I feel that this has happened to me. I don't understand it, but I love it. And I love you. And I thank you for sticking up for me and showing Busybody what was what."

Oh, go on! I'm blushing under my fur. Anyway, we'd better make a move.

Lily slammed the boot, walked the length of her car, and by the time she got behind the steering wheel, Seb was sitting in the passenger seat staring straight ahead as though ignoring her would make it okay. She didn't say a word, just got out of her side of the car, walked around to his, opened his door and pulled the seat belt around him, clicking it into place. He continued to ignore her. Maybe it was beneath his dignity to be strapped in, but she still wasn't going to risk sending him through the windscreen if she had to stop suddenly.

Of course, all that made her even later, and her father was waiting outside his house when she pulled up. He strode down the garden path and approached her car, incredulity writ large on his face. She wound her window down.

"Are you kidding me? You've got a dog? You know your mother doesn't like dogs."

"I haven't got him for her. I've got him for me."

I'm not anyone's.

"I don't like dogs either."

"He's not for you either. He's mine."

I'm not anyone's, although I don't mind you pretending I'm yours as a temporary measure.

"And you've belted him into his seat."

"I know I have."

"But he's a dog!"

"He's sitting in the front seat. He needs a belt on like anyone sitting in the front seat. Anyway, it's illegal to have a passenger in the front not strapped in."

"But he's a dog."

"I know."

"You can't bring him into the house."

"I'm not leaving him in the car. Someone might nick him."

Heck, heck, heck.

"He looks dangerous."

*I **am** dangerous. Dangerous as only a Sebastian Hound can be. Oh, yes!* He thrust his furry chest out and snorted.

"He's not dangerous. Not if you're nice to him."

"Bring him in then, but your mother won't like it."

Lily opened the car door and unclicked Seb's belt. He jumped out and stood very close to her father, staring at him, sniffing.

"What's he doing?" her father demanded.

"What are you doing?" she asked Seb.

I'm making him feel uncomfortable. He's not very nice is he? You'd have thought he'd be nicer to his own pup. Why does he talk to you as though you're an idiot? He doesn't like me staring at him and sniffing, does he? Most people don't.

"I'm not surprised," she said. "I wouldn't want a big black hairy dog staring at me and sniffing like that, either."

"Are you talking to this dog?" her father asked.

"Uh. Yes. You'd be surprised what he understands," she said, thinking she really had to be more careful.

"I see. So he understands you does he?" her father said in that tone of voice he had that suggested he was humouring her with his endless patience.

"Yes, he does," she said. "He understands every word I say." She just managed not to stick her tongue out. Her father always made her feel like she was a child again, regardless that she had left home and supported herself for the last six years.

"In that case, tell him to stop staring at me and sniffing! Oh, and then tell him to run around the lawn, take a drink out of the pond and pee on your mother's gentians." He laughed inordinately as though he'd told the joke of all time.

Lily ground her teeth.

Go on then. Tell me those things your sire said.

Reluctantly, Lily turned to Seb. He wasn't a ruddy circus dog. She didn't want to do this.

Oh, go on. I want to see his face.

"Are you sure you want him to pee on Mother's gentians?" Lily asked her father. "You know how possessive she is of them. I'll just tell him to do the other things and leave out the gentians bit shall I?"

"Don't be ridiculous. He's not going to do it anyway, and even if he chooses to pee on some plant or other, how would he know which ones were gentians?"

"He's a very clever dog," she said, conscious that her chin was jutting out and her voice childishly mutinous. "If you insist. On your head be it. I'll have to tell her you said so. I'm not taking the blame for damage to Mother's gentians."

The only answer she got was more of that bloody irritating laughter.

Go on then. I know my flowers, no bones there.

"Okay then, Dad. You asked for it," Lily said. "Now then, Seb…"

"Seb?" her father scoffed. "What a wimpish name for such a big dog!"

"It's not wimpish! It's short for Sebastian which means revered or majestic. Or both. And it means he's a fighter and strong and can rip the world apart with his teeth."

You're getting carried away now. How would I get my jaws around the world?

"Sebastian? Who in their right mind would call a mangy cur, Sebastian? You can't call a dog Sebastian!"

Lily sighed. Why did she let them get to her?

Why indeed?

She ignored his question. "Now then, Seb. Stop staring at Dad, run around the lawn, take a drink out of the pond and then have a pee on the gentians. There's a good dog."

Sausages for breakfast tomorrow?

"Crikey. I might have known. Yep. Sausages. And black pudding. And…"

I don't mind giving the black pudding a miss… Seb tore his gaze from Lily's father and cantered off. He ran around the perimeter of the closely shaved lawn, lapped at the pond until Lily was sure the fish would be left exposed and gasping for air on the banks, and then he headed for the gentians.

Glancing at her father she was most gratified to see that his mouth hung open in an oik kind of way and the colour had fled his cheeks. She battled with herself not to laugh. She must simply behave as though this was exactly what she had expected, and he should have too.

The front door opened and her mother appeared as if on cue – just as Seb lifted his leg and aimed a stream of golden liquid at her gentians.

"Hey," she screamed and raced across the lawn towards him. "Get this mongrel out of here. Look what he's doing to my gentians."

"Stop her Dad," Lily said. "My dog was told to do that. I can't have Mother threatening him. I don't know what he'd do and I have to keep discipline. He can't be told off for doing as he's told."

The colour returned to her father's face in an avalanche of puce and he muttered something indistinguishable before striding over to his wife. He caught her arm raised in menace at the dog and pulled her away.

"John! Stop that dog. Look what he's doing. My poor gentians won't survive under that onslaught."

Seb did seem to be going on a bit, Lily thought.

Got a lot of pond water to get rid of.

Lily couldn't hear what her father said to her mother but she could tell by their posture that Words Would Be Had later.

She wandered over. "Hello Mum," she said.

Her mother looked at her for a while saying nothing and then turned and marched into the house.

Lily'd had more affectionate greetings from her mother over the years. But not often.

Why didn't you tell me she's not your mother?

"Pardon?"

She's not your mother.

"What are you blathering on about?" she demanded of him.

"Are you talking to that dog again?" her father asked. "I wish you wouldn't, Lily. It makes me uncomfortable. You could get in trouble."

"Trouble? Why would I get in trouble?"

He pulled on his collar and wouldn't look directly at her. "People wouldn't like it. People have been locked up for less."

"For talking to their dogs? You're kidding me. What's wrong with talking to your dog?"

"Nothing, I suppose," he said grudgingly. "The trouble arises when you tell people he's talking back and that you understand what he's saying." He gave her such a quelling look Lily hesitated to pursue the subject any further.

Just as well. Not everyone needs to know.

"Okay. I've brought the cards I promised, Dad. Maybe I'd better leave you to mollify Mum."

She leaned in to kiss him and he swayed towards her as if by accident. At least he didn't turn away. They'd never been a huggy-kissy family, but she was trying to be more openly affectionate these days. She had friends who unselfconsciously hugged everyone. That wasn't the way she'd been brought up, but she thought it would be nice if they could be more like that.

In the car again Lily got the third degree from Seb.

What are those cards?

"They're some of mine. That I've designed and had printed."

You're an artist?

"Yep. That's right."

Bones! What do you paint?

Lily paused. She just knew he was going to make something of this.

What? What?

"I paint dogs."

You paint dogs! See, I knew there had to be some reason I'd been sent to you specifically.

"What do you mean?"

I didn't turn up on your doorstep by accident, you know. There must have been a reason, and now I know you paint dogs, that must be it.

She glanced at him and hastily back at the road again. "What would that be, then?"

You must be meant to paint me. Lots of pictures of me. That'll be it.

They were home now, and parked up. Lily had released his seat belt and could see Seb grinning all over his furry face at the idea. She supposed it might be useful to have her own model for her pics instead of having to take photos of friends' dogs, or finding pictures online that didn't have copyright clauses attached to them. It could be useful.

Of course it will be. That must be why I'm here.

"So what was that fight about last night?"

Oh, that. I shouldn't worry about that. That's just something else we have to deal with while we're here.

"We?"

My queen and me. By the way, her name's not really Caramel Girl but you wouldn't be able to pronounce her Realm name, so it'll do.

"You came together? Why aren't you together now? Why did she go to Rude Git's place and not to me, then?"

I don't know. I'm just a lowly warrior Hound. My queen tells me what to do and I do it without question. And we might have come to the Human Territories together but she knew where she was going, whereas I took a while to find you.

"You do what your queen tells you without question? That explains why you argue with everyone else!"

I do not! Heck, heck, heck.

"And, just by the way, what was all that about my mother not being my mother?"

He turned to her, a bewildered look on his face, his tongue fell out of his mouth and he woofed around it. It came out sounding like: *wylliffll*.

Lily wasn't fooled by his dumb-dog act, not for a minute! "Come **on**. What did you mean?"

I don't think I should have said anything, now that I think about it. Humans are a bit weird about these things aren't they?

"What did you mean?"

She didn't smell like she should.

Inexplicably relieved, Lily laughed. "Is that all? I'm not surprised she didn't smell like she should – she's always doing something or other that involves not smelling like herself – having her hair dyed, getting massaged with strange-smelling unguents, spraying herself with stuff to make **sure** she doesn't smell of herself. I'm surprised she smells at all human. Some people do that to their dogs, too. They don't want them to smell like dogs. They'd rather they smelled of lavender or baby powder. Human baby powder, that is."

Seb stiffened in his seat, turning to her, eyes round with horror. *What!!! What happens to the dog? Do they have identity problems? How can they tell what they are if they can't smell themselves smelling like themselves?*

"I don't know. I've only **heard** that people do that," Lily said, a bit taken aback. "I've never had a dog myself."

You've never had a dog! Impossibly, he looked even more horrified and launched himself across the gear stick at her. Squashed between the steering wheel and Lily, Seb's weight appeared to increase and Lily, although grateful for such concern and affection, couldn't breathe. She pummelled his back until he moved. While she gulped down great lungfuls of air, Seb contented himself with licking her hand. It was making her skin itch, but she didn't have the heart to stop him.

Eventually, they exited the car, though, when they saw Busybody heading towards them, and raced into the house giggling and wuffling.

Lily had more cards to pack and they settled in the study, whereupon Seb gave Lily a caution about openly talking to him. *See the way Busybody was looking at you? Well, some people will get scared if they think you're talking to your dog, and scared people are unpredictable. So, be a bit careful because most humans don't talk with their dogs, most aren't capable of it and most of their dogs aren't capable of it either.*

"How come I can, then?" Lily wanted to know.

You're special. Seb levered himself up and wandered off, sniffing noisily at a trail only he perceived. It seemed to lead towards the kitchen. What a surprise!

Lily stopped, envelope inside the greeting card, cellophane bag ready to receive both. She was special. He'd said she was special and he'd said it in such a way that it was simply a fact, not a big deal. Just a fact. Tears jumped to her eyes but she willed them away. If Seb could be that casual about calling her special in that matter-of-fact way, then she could be that casual about accepting it.

Except she couldn't. Had anyone ever called her special before? She couldn't think anyone ever had.

There's much stupidity about.

She flinched. Seb was at her elbow. She must get used to the fact that she had an ever-present eavesdropper on her thoughts.

Eavesdropper? Not at all. Hearing all your thoughts is purely by the way. Guardian would be a better term. I need to know what you're thinking so I can protect you before you even know you need it. Anyway, you'll soon learn how to guard your thoughts from me and from anyone else.

"Uh, we haven't exactly established what I need protecting against yet, have we? Shall we do that?"

Hmmm. He gave it some thought. *Nah.*

He wandered off again and she could hear him poking about in the kitchen. Although he hadn't yet worked out how to open the fridge, she could clearly hear the cupboard doors slamming and a lot of snuffling noises.

"But what if I see one of those patches of greyness?" She raised her voice to make sure he heard her. "That thing you and Caramel Girl were fighting. What was that? In fact, I think I just saw one go past the window."

And suddenly she was fighting for breath with a mouthful of fur and a heaving chest pressed against her face and the weight of his front paws on her thigh as he squashed his nose against the window. *Where? Where? Where is it? What did you see? How many? Where?*

"I was joking," she choked, spitting out dog hairs and trying to get away from his erratically thundering heart. "I was joking!"

It's no joking matter, young pup! And he swiped her across the ear with his raspy old paw. It felt like she'd lost several layers of skin. *The Crules are nothing to joke about! Don't ever do that again!* He gave her a close-up of his teeth, lowered himself to the floor leaving what felt like great craters in her thighs where his paws had been, and hopped up on the sofa. He appeared to have a huge frown on his brow.

"No dogs on the furniture," she said, trying not to feel like she'd been told off. "This is a no-dogs-on-the furniture household." Never mind that no dogs had ever been in this house – at least while she'd been in it.

But the look Seb gave her made her think that maybe Majestic Hounds should be allowed. After all, not many of them came along in a lifetime.

Stop worrying about one or two Sebastian Hound hairs on the furniture, and start worrying about why I'm here.

"If only I **knew** why you were here, I'm sure I'd have plenty to worry about," she said.

He gave her a considering look as if trying to work out if she could cope with the truth. *I'm not really a dog as such. Well, I **am** a dog, but really I'm a Seb Hound. A Sebastian Hound. We are the majestic. We are the guardians of the Realm. This means that if we leave the Realm it must be very important indeed.*

"I thought Seb was your **name**," she said, clutching at the only thing she could make any sense of.

*Nah. Not exactly. It's what I **am**. A Seb Hound. Short for Sebastian Hound. My real name is unpronounceable by humans. I can't even spell it in a way you would recognise. So keep calling me Seb. Caramel Girl is our Supremity, our Sovereign, to use an expression you would know. I don't know how to explain the real word for her. She is peerless. She is what keeps the Realm intact. She is what holds us all together and makes sense of our existence. She is the epitome of Good. She is the very air we breathe, the strength of purity, the perfume on the breeze of life, the softness of a loving smile, the...*

"And you're in love with her," Lily said, interrupting him before he started to drool.

Great bones! Of course I'm not. I love her like we all do. But I am merely a Seb Hound. I cannot dream inappropriately of our Supremity. I would be banished to wander the Void of Nothingness forever, where all is grey and pointless, until I, too, became empty and indifferent, sucked dry of everything that matters.

"Blimey. I thought this Realm of yours was a good place. That's a pretty naff thing to do to someone."

I might have been exaggerating. He grinned and it was just as well she recognised his grin now or she'd have wet herself with fright at the ivory weapons of mass destruction now on show.

"So, what would happen if she knew you were in love with her?"

*I wouldn't ever put her in the position of knowing. Uh – not that I **am** in love with her, of course. I wouldn't ever want to make her feel awkward. It is my duty to keep it to myself and not burden anyone else with it. I'll expect you to keep your ideas to yourself about it, too, young pup.*

"Oy! What's with this 'young pup' business? I'll have you know I'm twenty-four. I'm old. I'm an adult. And I don't need my ears smacked, thank you!"

Behave like a young pup, and I'll treat you like a young pup. Twenty-four is old, is it? Heck, heck, heck.

"How old are you then? I can't tell under all that fur."

Our years aren't the same as yours but I'm older than you. I'm older than an old oak, older than an old turtle, older than an old leepig, older than you. Not that you're as old as an old turtle, but...

"What's a leepig? Oh, and what's a Crule?"

But the door knocker banging startled them both. Seb leapt up and stiffened into fighting stance. Lily leapt up and hesitated. There was no telling what was out there these days.

You're right to be wary. I should have warned you about...

More banging drowned the rest out, or had he suddenly stopped talking to her? She wasn't sure, but Lily rushed off and answered the door to stop the racket, although she opened it slowly with her foot behind it and peered through the crack like a frightened little old lady worried about door-step muggers. However, the sight of an elderly man in a hat, full three-piece suit, complete with collar and tie, had her throwing the door wide and smiling at him. He reminded her of her granddad. Sadly, he died when she was very little. "Hello," she said.

He removed his hat. "I'm so sorry to bother you but my wife is distraught. We lost our dog last night in the storm. He got frightened and ran away when we let him out into the garden last thing to do his business. We're going around the neighbourhood knocking on doors to see if anyone's taken him in. Have you seen a dog?"

Lily's guilt mechanism immediately whizzed around at full blast. She just knew she'd stolen this elderly couple's treasured pet. She was also sure that anyone could see at a glance that she was guilty as sin.

"Uh. What does he look like?"

"He's big and black and very hairy, but really he's a softie at heart." The man chuckled fondly and Lily felt herself being put at her ease. She relaxed until she realised that she was indeed being put at her ease by something other than herself. It was as though someone had thrown a soft blanket over her nerves and forced them to smooth out, like someone was controlling her. Not at all like Seb's invasion of her mind which felt natural. Talking of which, why wasn't Seb communicating with her any more, telling her what to do?

What if she really had fallen over, bashed her head and hallucinated the whole talking-dog thing? She had a very sore palm to show that she had fallen over. She even glanced down at it. And the dog she had in the house behind her was this man and his wife's much-loved but missing pooch. She imagined Mrs Three-piece-suit crying into an ironed, rose-perfumed lace hankie at home, inconsolable at the loss of her pet. Why wasn't Seb talking to her if she hadn't imagined all the Seb Hound stuff? Lily felt cold and alone without him hovering in her mind.

Even so, she said: "I'm sorry, but I've not seen such a dog." She gazed at Mr Three-piece-suit and tried very hard to keep her face blank but she felt sick. She felt guilty. And why had she lied? Why couldn't Seb be the missing pet? Surely he must *be* the missing pet... Mr Three-piece-suit darted forward much faster than she would have thought possible for someone as seemingly decrepit as him and snatched at her sweater. She jumped back in fright, and, about to yell at him for his nerve, she realised he was holding up a long black hair. His look bored through her. Was it her over-vivid imagination again, or did his eyes look as though they had no pupils?

Her own hair was chestnut and nowhere on her head could be found a hair that length. That was a very long hair. Just exactly like Seb's.

Startling herself out of her temporary paralysis she leaned against the door frame, folded her arms in what she hoped was a very casual way, and said, "Oh, yes, that's Monty's. That's my dog's. The house is covered in them. Honestly, it's like his stuffing is coming out. All the time. Still, it's free insulation. Free sound-proofing. Ha ha ha."

She would have thought that went quite well except her last laugh broke and fell on the floor, whimpered, struggled feebly and then died. And she still couldn't understand why she was automatically lying to this poor old man about a dog that she had indeed found just last night, but somehow she couldn't find the truth within her. Or not to share with Mr Three-piece-suit anyway, no matter how much he looked like her granddad. Somehow she knew she was right to lie.

And where the flaming hell had the name 'Monty' come from? How had it got into her brain?

Mr Three-piece-suit said, "May I see him? May I see Monty?" He said it in such a soothing voice that Lily found herself turning to call for Monty, but she realised, once again, that she was being manipulated somehow. She wrenched her mind back to herself and said, "Why? He's *my* Monty-Dog. Why do you want to see him?" She stuck her chin out and channelled belligerence. Not that it was that difficult. She was beginning to get a bit ratty with old Three-piece-suit.

He gazed at her, his eyes hardening, his wrinkles disappearing, or was she imagining that? Fear swept through her as he opened his mouth, but was jolted away as a disturbance in the hall behind her registered on her consciousness. She turned around to see what was going on and her Monty-Dog appeared. It had to be her imaginary Monty-Dog because it certainly wasn't a Seb Hound! Surreptitiously, she pinched the back of her left hand to make sure she was awake. It hurt, which was the idea, but she still saw an imaginary Monty-Dog and not a Seb Hound.

This dog was bowling down the hall. He looked as though he was wrestling with himself, his tail held firmly in his mouth, his eyes rolling wildly. Transfixed, Lily simply stood there. How could this be possible? She didn't have a Monty-Dog. She'd never had a dog. There was only a Seb Hound in her house. Where was he? Lily looked over Monty-Dog's shoulder but couldn't see Seb. There was just this Monty-Dog behaving like a half-wit right in front of her eyes. She *must* be hallucinating now!

"Monty-Dog!" she quavered, coughed, and tried again. "Monty!" She plastered on a doting smile and held her hand out to him.

Monty stopped growling at his own paw, which part of his anatomy was now clenched between magnificent teeth, cocked an eyebrow at her, wagged his tail furiously, dropped his limb, sprang to his feet and bounded over to her like a puppy. She wondered if her hands would pass straight through him, but no, they clasped fur-covered muscle. His breath was sweeter than Seb's by a mile. No sausage-breath here!

She had no idea what was going on, but it was lovely to be so close to a creature so happy! There had been few happy creatures in her life. Lily fought with herself not to cry. That would probably puzzle Mr Three-piece-suit mightily given this was supposed to be her dog, her constant, everyday companion. If she was still suffering concussion, and hallucinating all this, it was so worth it!

She leaned over Monty-Dog to get her arms around as much of him as possible, and hugged him hard; he laid his head lovingly on her shoulder. Her composure recovered, she straightened up to look at Mr Three-piece-suit who surveyed Monty with an expression Lily could only describe as thwarted. But he still stood there, making no move to leave. Surely he needed to get around as many houses as possible to find his missing dog.

"Well, there you go. That's my Monty-Dog. He's obviously not your dog. I wish you the best of luck finding your dog. It must be so awful to lose a pet like that."

"How long have you had him?" The question shot at her as though from a crossbow.

Lily couldn't think what to say. She didn't want to be rude, but nor was she prepared to answer questions that were nothing to do with anyone else but herself. Monty-Dog ambled forward, snuffled around Mr Three-piece-suit's feet, got himself in position, and lifted his leg.

"Oh, my goodness!" Lily cried and lunged for his collar to drag him back, whereupon a stream of pee drenched her door frame. Nice.

"What a stupid mutt!" Mr Three-piece-suit yelled. "That can't possibly be my dog!"

"You mean you couldn't tell just by looking?" Lily snapped.

He gave her a fierce glare and stomped off without shutting the garden gate. Fancy a dog owner not shutting a gate!!! He no longer reminded her of her granddad either. Her granddad was a much nicer man, sadly missed.

Once more back in the house, after she'd poured a bucket of water over the door frame to rinse it off, she regarded Monty-Dog. Where had Seb gone? Or had he morphed into Monty-Dog? Would he morph back again?

"Are you Seb, really?" she asked him, but got no reply.

Was it all in her mind? She was too tired to care any more. It was what it was. She slumped down on the floor and putting her arms around Monty-Dog she laid her head on his side and relaxed.

When she surfaced it was to a message in her mind: *You've got a really heavy head, did you know that?*

She lifted her really heavy head off his chest and peered up at the face above her. It was Seb. Lily sat up and looked around. "Monty!" she yelled. "Monty-Dog!" But there was no sound of paws coming her way. No bark to announce a dog's arrival.

It was me.

"Are you a shape shifter as well, then?"

No, not really. It's about illusion. Maybe a little bit shape-shifterish as well...

"Why did you stop talking to me? It was as if you'd switched off. It left this cold bit in my head where you'd previously been. It left me adrift."

Sorry about that. I hadn't been expecting a Crule to turn up on your doorstep. I still don't understand why he did. But the thing about the Crules, and the Crules-in-training, is that they can sense someone broadcasting, so I had to stop the second I knew he was there. I had to be guarded so as not to attract any more of them. He was looking for me. That Crule turned up just when we were about to have a chat about the Crules so I didn't have a chance to explain them before you were confronted with one, but you did very well.

"Probably because I didn't know he was a Crule! If I'd known I'd probably have been too frightened to do anything!"

Heck, heck.

"I thought the Crules were things like that evil thing you and Caramel Girl were fighting last night. That person at the door looked like my grandfather at the start of it. At the end he didn't look so nice."

You have a grandsire?

"Not any more. He was my father's father, but he died a long time ago. He was nice."

What about your mother's sire?

"He died before I was born. Why?"

Just trying to sort your family out. To get back to the Crules – they can also do the illusion thing, with a bit of shape-shifterishness thrown in when it suits them. But I could smell he was a Crule.

"Does that mean he could smell you were a Sebastian Hound?"

I don't think Crules smell anything. They smell **of** *plenty. But they don't smell so much as sense things. And I was completely guarded. He wouldn't be able to sense me. If he had, he wouldn't have been fooled by the Monty-Dog incarnation.*

"Who is Monty-Dog, anyway?"

He's a dog who used to live in this house. He offered me his services when he realised what was happening.

"A ghost-dog? Now you're **really** asking me to believe too much!"

Not a ghost like humans think of them, but a presence, if you like.

Lily decided to let it pass. Her head was already having trouble getting itself around talking dogs and shape-shifters without worrying about ghost-dogs as well. "So, in words of one syllable, what is a Crule?"

It's a human being gone bad.

"As in **gone off**, do you mean?" she said. "Heck, heck."

Seb merely stared at her until she stopped grinning and started feeling foolish.

They are not funny. Nothing about them is funny. They have no compassion, no feeling for others, no interests except their own.

"It didn't look very human last night."

Once they're that bad they can be difficult to recognise. They usually present to the world the image they want seen at that time. However, there are millions of Crules-in-training slinking around the Human Territories —that is, your world —so you need to be careful. Just as well you've got me now to keep an eye out for you.

Lily tried for a grateful smile, but it faltered and died before fruition.

Seb patted her with one of his enormous paws. *You must always try to think good thoughts; it's much more difficult for a Crule to get you then. And it'll be a good start*

44

to learning how to guard yourself. Consciously thinking good things makes it much more difficult for anything bad to sneak in.

Lily sighed. Suddenly life had become incredibly awkward.

We're here, Caramel Girl and me, because we were attacked by Crules years ago in the Realm. We had to throw them out. In doing so, we threw out all our Compeers as well.

"Compeers? What are Compeers?"

Seb cocked his head to one side. *Um. I'm pretty certain that's a human word, so you should know. Compeers are, um, like friends. But we can't live properly without them although we have tried since the Great Betrayal.*

"The Great Betrayal?" Lily queried, but as she did so, she felt there to be something familiar about the phrase although she couldn't think what. It made her uneasy so she changed the subject. "Can't live without each other? What, you mean like a symbiotic relationship?" She studied her nails very casually trying not to look smug. She knew the term because she'd recently read a book about sea anemones that rode around the oceans on the back of hermit crabs, and birds that ate the ticks off the backs of some animals like zebras and elephants.

Yep, that's right, oh, Smug One. Like that. Our Compeers. You might be my Compeer. I don't know. I've never had one. They were all thrown out in my grandsire's time. But we need to get them back before we die out altogether. We are not thriving alone. We were never meant to. Talking of not thriving – I think it's time for sausages. I need sausages to keep going. It's been a hard couple of hours since the last sausage ration.

For a large Sebastian Hound he did a very good job of looking malnourished and unloved. Lily heaved herself to her feet and made for the kitchen with a large, malnourished and unloved Sebastian Hound dogging her footsteps all the way. "Yep. We need to keep our strength up."

Yep. Got lots of strength to keep up. Yep.

"Then we've got to get around to Rude Git's place and sort out a few things." Lily saw Seb's ears go up and she stopped shifting the sausages around in the pan long enough to wave the frying slice at him. "Look at you," she said gleefully. "The thought of seeing Caramel Girl and you've come over all bright-eyed and spiky-furred."

He stared at her unblinkingly. *Where are my sausages, oh Sausage-Cooker?*

She smacked him with the frying slice and he leapt back yelping in terror. Lily's remorse went off the clock before she realised he was near-as-dammit sniggering at her. So she smacked him again.

Oy!

"Serves you right."

It was funny, the way you thought you'd hurt me. Me – a Sebastian Hound hurt by a fly-swatter. Heck, heck, heck.

"I know what you're doing. You're trying to get me off the subject of you and Caramel Girl. You can't fool me, you know. Or, not for long."

Where are my sausages???

Bowing to the inevitable, Lily loaded up his plate with the best of the shop's sausages, in this case, pork and Stilton. She'd thrown together some bubble and squeak to go with them. This met with great Sebastian Hound approval. Lily beamed at him while he scoffed the lot with barely a pause. A large burp resounded around the house when he'd finished and he subsided in a replete heap on the floor. But it wasn't long before the gargantuan meal had apparently been absorbed into his system and he sat up and fixed her with his beady eyes.

We'd better get around there before the day runs out. Come on!

They set off. There was a light breeze. The sun shone. It was a nice day for a walk. Except they were going to Rude Git's house. Lily's feet dragged a little.

Come on. We need to get there so we can plan things.

"Plan what things?"

We have to have reconciliation with our former Compeers and their descendants and we have to get them home to the Realm. They were all thrown out after the Great Betrayal. Now we must get them back. For their sake as well as ours.

Lily felt that unease again on hearing the expression: 'Great Betrayal', but she was still puzzled as to why she should.

You're the One Who Knows. You should know.

"I'm the One Who Knows what?"

How am I supposed to know what you know. You're the One Who Knows that.

"Why am I the One Who Knows?"

I don't know why you're the One Who Knows. But the Ageless Chronicles say it is so. Unfortunately, they were also a casualty of the Wars of the Great Betrayal and so they only remain in fragments, but there is a fragment that states that the One Who Knows will be the key to healing the Realm. But first must come reconciliation.

"How can that have been written down *before* the Wars of the Great Betrayal? How would they have known the Realm needing healing?"

Oh, young pup. You have much to learn! They're not written down – they are kept in the consciousness of the Ageless Ones – that is the reason for their existence – to keep the memory of everything forever. That's why they are immortal. They also know what's going to happen before it happens but in such a way that it only makes sense after it's happened. We used to have an Ageless Panacea One who could work some of it out, which was helpful, but we no longer have her either.

He stopped to sniff at a lamp post, but apparently didn't find it appealing and carried on.

The Ageless Ones keep the Chronicles, and eat clawkle, of course. That's what actually makes them immortal.

"How come it's in fragments, then, if it's not written down? And what happened to the Ageless Panacea One? And what the hell is clawkle?"

Some of our Ageless Ones were lost in the Void, including, we think, the Panacea One. Ageless Ones are the same as Crules in that they cannot be killed. But they can be lost in the Void. Hence, we only have some fragments of some Chronicles, including the one about the One Who Knows. And clawkle is a drug. It's used for good and for evil, same as any drug. But I don't think the clawkle vine grows here.

"How do you know I'm the One Who Knows? I might not be her." Lily couldn't help wishing she **wasn't** the One Who Knows. It sounded a horribly responsible thing to be. She could barely drag herself through each day, only to find another day to drag herself through, let alone have to be responsible for a whole Realm!

Caramel Girl knows you're the One Who Knows.

He made this pronouncement so matter-of-factly, Lily didn't bother to argue. "Oh, well. I **must** be the One Who Knows, then," she muttered.

Yep. So you're the one to sort out the reconciliation thing and save our world. That's between the Great Betrayer and the Greatly Betrayed, before you ask.

"I have to be a negotiator between this Betrayer and the Betrayed?"

Yep. Something like that. You'll be fine.

Lily stopped walking. A little old lady with a trolley swore at her in unexpectedly colourful fashion, and overtook, looking back with evil glances. "Except I haven't a clue who is which and how to do it," Lily wailed. "How could I possibly know what to do? I never even knew there was another world out there, the Realm. I've never known about the Crules. How could I know?" Lily was horrified to think that a world might be lost because she didn't know what she was supposed to know. Crikey. It was the story of her life according to her parents. She never did do what she was supposed to do and here she was doing it again. Or rather, not doing it again.

Don't be silly. We know you know. You don't know you know but that doesn't matter. We know you know. We just have to think of a way of making you find out how to know what we need you to know.

Seb looked at her, complete confidence shining from his eyes and Lily wanted to cry. She was so unaccustomed to anyone having confidence in her.

It's very odd. Why is that? You're a lovely person. You've started and built up your own business which must be going well if you own your own kennel and eat sausages all the time. Food of the Dogs, they are, so why are you regarded as a failure? Or maybe you're not and you just think that's what people think. Anyway, come on. We've got to get going.

Seb trotted ahead, but Lily didn't want to go. She felt bad enough already, without having to see Rude Git again. He would make her feel worse, for sure.

No he won't. He's part of it.

"Part of what?"

He's part of the whole thing. That's why Princess is there.

"Princess?"

Seb stopped so suddenly Lily fell over him. Whilst on the ground he took the opportunity to stare into her eyes at short range.

Princess. My princess. Our princess. The princess with a name there is no human equivalent word for, otherwise known to you as Caramel Girl.

"She's your princess?"

Yes! Of course she's my princess! Seb's breath came out in a huff with his vehemence, and Lily leapt to her feet scrabbling at her face. "Ohmigod. Your sausage-breath has stuck to my skin! Aarghh!"

Seb was singularly unimpressed with Lily's desperate attempts to wipe sausage-breath off herself. *Of course she's my princess. Couldn't you tell just by looking at her?*

He seemed really impatient with her short-sightedness.

"Give me a chance. Last night I didn't even know about the Realm, and the Crules, and Sebastian Hounds or this quest we're on, or anything. I certainly wasn't on the lookout for a strawberries and cream princess. Anyway, I had a Rude Git to contend with if you remember!"

Strawberries and cream. Heck. That's a good one. Strawberries and cream. She'll like that. I'll tell her that one. She is lovely isn't she?

"She certainly looked very pretty and she seemed like a very good natured dog, er princess, as well."

Lily watched as Seb tripped over nothing and had to gallop along a few paces to keep from falling on his face.

"You **are** in love with her aren't you?" she said gleefully.

I am not.

"Yes you are!"

Am not.

"Yes you are! You're blushing. I can tell."

He stopped and turned to her staring at her so hard she knew she was supposed to feel intimidated like her father had. She grinned at him. "Hehe. You can't fool me. I know you. You're in love with her. Anyway, I'm the One Who Knows. So I know! So there!"

He turned away and, tail down, he slogged along, saying nothing.

"Well, what's wrong with that? What's wrong with being in love with her?"

Nothing. We don't have a class system like you humans do. So no problems there…

"We don't have a class system!" Seb merely looked at her and Lily shut up.

Look at me. And then look at her. Why should she even look at me? I don't know if I'm a steady enough character for her. She has to rule the Realm, when we've saved it. She will be full of duty and responsibility and I'll still want to run wild and gallop with the wind, and jump in the Swirling Lake and swing over the falls on the Vines of Chance, and chase the leepigs.

"Chase the leepigs? Poor leepigs!"

It's a game. Leepigs like being chased. That's what they live for. They're always coming up to the dens and yowling for us to go out and chase them. Always.

"Leepig isn't another name for a cat is it?" Lily asked suspiciously.

Certainly not! Cats don't like being chased do they? He gave her a very withering look. *The point is, could I buckle down and always be a good and dutiful Sebastian Hound, or would I go off the rails? When I'm with her I have no doubts in my mind at all, but when I'm not it's different.*

"Does she love you?"

I don't know. She loves everyone, that's the trouble. Everyone. How is a Hound to know for sure?

"Ask her."

If the last withering look made her falter mid-stride, this one made her stumble back a pace or two, before she recovered enough to carry on – without saying another word.

Chapter Five

She'd rung the bell some time ago. Lily stood in front of his door remembering just how rude Rude Git was. As the door continued to remain shut she looked around her and marvelled at how normal everything looked in the light of day – how normal it all looked even though she was now talking to the animals…

Only to me.

Even though she was now talking to a dog about how to save a world and fight off unimaginable threats. And yet, look, people around the place were just doing ordinary things like mowing their lawns and cleaning their cars and walking down the road carrying shopping bags. Just ordinary things. It did make her wonder if she had actually hit her head and was lying in a coma in hospital dreaming all this.

Explain this!

Seb jumped up and huffed sausage-breath right in her face. Yep. That was real enough! Lily recoiled and fell over, arms flailing, desperately trying to keep her balance. The door opened and she fell into Rude Git, who didn't move. She didn't exactly bounce off him, but nearly. Hastily she pulled away. "Sorry. Sorry," she said, patting his chest nervously as though that would make it better.

Heck. Heck.

"And to what do I owe the pleasure?" Rude Git enquired in a voice that made it obvious that 'the pleasure' was another way of saying 'dog turd'.

But maybe that was just his manner, Lily thought. She couldn't launch an attack on him for his tone of voice if he couldn't help his tone of voice. Maybe he always sounded like he had a dog turd under his nose. She stifled an inappropriate giggle.

"We've come to…" Cripes. What *have* we come to do?

We've come to see Princess and plan how to save the Realm.

I'll try that then shall I? "We came to see Amber," Lily faltered, not quite able to look him in the face and checking out his rather nice cashmere jumper just inches from her nose instead. It was in lovely shades of heather.

"She's fine. You don't need to see her. She's *my* dog and I'm looking after her perfectly well. Which is more than can be said for you after you let your dog attack my dog last night."

She's not anybody's dog!

"I did not! My dog did *not* attack your dog!" Lily snapped.

"Why do you want to see her anyway? Do you usually call on other people's dogs? That's a bit odd isn't it?"

Oh, if only you knew, Lily thought. If only you really, really knew what 'odd' was!

*She doesn't **belong** to anyone!*

Rude Git carried on: "So, what's the *real* reason for your visit?" He looked the picture of suspicion with narrowed eyes and twisted lips. They could be quite nice lips, actually, if they were less sneery and more smiley.

"Well?" he demanded, jerking Lily from her reverie.

"Just to see Amber," She said firmly. What else could she possibly say?

I've had enough of this. You humans waste so much time!

And Seb charged between Rude Git and the door frame and cantered off down the hallway.

"Hey!" Rude Git shouted after him. Turning back to Lily he said, "Have you no control over that dog at all? At the very least you should go to obedience classes if you're going to have a dog. You can't let him do what he likes. I suppose you'd better come in now in order to get him out."

Grudgingly he stepped back and Lily surged forward. She'd had warmer welcomes in her life, but she was on a mission now. She had a world to save and Rude Git wasn't going to put her off. She followed Seb down the hall to find both dogs ensconced in front of the Aga, heads together, no doubt conspiring. She regarded them suspiciously.

We've had a quick chat. The first thing to do is get Rude Git to believe that he and Caramel Girl can talk to each other.

"Oh, piece of cake then," she muttered.

Great! I love cake!

"No, I mean... Oh, never mind." She realised Rude Git was watching her, a sour expression ageing his face.

"Listen," she said. "I don't think we got off to a very good start..."

"You don't think?"

"Er, no. We didn't. But we could try again."

"Why?"

"Because... we... are..." she tried desperately to think of something to say. There was no good reason for this man to have to tolerate her or her dog in his house.

Oy!

Well, no good reason that he would believe.

"Because?" Rude Git prompted.

"Because my dog has, er... fallen in love with your dog. I mean, just look at them." She gestured wildly towards the happy couple by the stove. Seb looked embarrassed, Lily was sure of it. Caramel Girl smiled, and she stretched out her nose to rest it on Seb's front paw. Lily thought she winked at her and she grinned. Seb looked even more uncomfortable.

Hmphh.

"Dogs don't fall in love," Rude Git said. "Don't give them human attributes. It's silly and a waste of my time!"

"How can you be so certain of that?" To think that she'd have probably agreed with him a couple of days ago, but this Rude Git **needed** arguing with!

The look he gave her could have dissolved granite. "They're **dogs**," he said, as though that would forever put paid to any argument.

"Being a dog is not a reason," Lily said.

"Of course it is. And even if they did, uh... **fall in love**, and even if these two had, the only thing to do would be to have them fixed – there are quite enough unwanted dogs in the world as it is, and we don't want to add to their number. Oh my god, what am I doing arguing with you over something this bloody stupid? What are you doing here, apart from wasting my time and trying my patience?"

Fixed? What does he mean? Not what I think he means, I hope.

Lily could see Seb's outrage quivering in the air, but despite it, she knew she must ignore it. She had very little time before Rude Git physically threw her out and there were important things to achieve before that happened.

"The thing is," she said. "That you and your dog could communicate if only you would open yourself up to her."

He scowled and Lily's heart stuttered. He looked so stunningly handsome. He should be striding across a moor, a Golden Eagle on his wrist, thunderclouds piling up behind him, but not daring to drop any rain on his head, lightning lighting up the sky, but not daring to strike him; the world still and empty, simply waiting for him.

Did she have her mouth open? She had her mouth open. Oh, no! She slammed it shut.

"You're not that bloody dog psychobabble therapist who's been trying to get an appointment for the last week, are you? You must be. Well, you can sod right off!"

"I'm not a dog psychologist, but even if I were – what's wrong with that? Dogs have mental needs as well as physical ones. Surely you'd admit that."

The look on his face made her hurry on. "Even so, the point is that you must listen to your dog."

She's not anyone's dog.

"You must listen to Caramel Girl…"

"Amber!"

Lily ignored the interruption. "She has a world to save. Her world. Her world and all the Hounds and the Compeers. It will all be destroyed by humans gone bad if we don't do something to save it."

His face suddenly cleared and hope sprang alive in Lily's chest. Rude Git took her by the arm and led her to the table, pushing her down into a chair. He put the kettle on.

Thank heaven for that. He was going to listen. Lily could have wept with relief.

"You poor girl. Did you fall last night as well? I know you did, because of the state of your palm. How is it by the way? I think you must have hit your head as well. But," he held up his hands as if she'd been about to argue, "…don't worry. We'll get you sorted out. Just sit there, have a cup of tea and I'll take you to the hospital. You'll need an x-ray first, maybe a scan. But whatever it is, we can cope with this. I've got the time to help. Surgery for this morning is over and it's not open again until this evening. Is there someone you'd like me to ring?"

Come **on**. *You're the One Who Knows. Get him to believe. You can do this.*

She didn't feel like she could do this at all.

"Listen," Rude Git said. "We've not properly been introduced. My name is Matt Lannings. I'm a vet." When she still said nothing, he prompted her: "And… you… are..?" he said it slowly and clearly as if she were a very young child from a different country, or someone who'd been hit on the head and couldn't think straight. He clearly believed he was dealing with the second option.

Lily sighed. She had the feeling it was going to be a long, frustrating afternoon.

You can do it!

How can a dog smirk? She was sure that's what he was doing. By this time both Caramel Girl and Seb had their heads resting on their paws. Lily wished she could rest **her** head on her paws as well, preferably in bed at home.

"My name is Lily Wilkins. I design and produce greeting cards."

He gave her an encouraging smile and she melted for a second before girding herself again. He was trying to convince her that she didn't know what she knew. But she did know what she knew. Apart from anything else, she was the One Who Knows!

Yep. That's you. Yep.

She pulled her shoulders back and faced him squarely. "Matt," she said. "It is really important that you listen to me about this. There is a Realm in peril, a whole race of people, or rather, Hounds, and people, too, if you count the Compeers, in trouble from a network of Crules both here and there, and..."

He grabbed her hand and held it in both of his. He had such an earnest expression on his face that she almost wanted to be as unbalanced as he thought she was. But she wasn't. She pulled her hand from his. "You have to listen to me," she said.

In response he gripped his own hands together. Lily could tell by the way parts of them went white that he was trying to keep his patience. Trying very, very hard.

Tell him something you can't possibly know. That'll convince him.

"Like what?" she demanded, giving up all pretence of **not** talking to the dog now. "Tell him what?"

"Yes, tell me what?" Matt said.

"Seb has suggested that if I tell you something I can't possibly know then you'll believe that I can communicate with him, and by the same token you can communicate with Caramel Girl."

"Amber."

"Amber."

"Go on, then. Tell me something you can't possibly know. I'm all agog." He folded his arms. A sure sign that his agogness wasn't as receptive as one might expect an agogness to be.

Lily turned to Seb, turned back to Matt and said: "I can't possibly know that you had a jumper that you wore just for gardening. It was one of those really bad Christmas sweaters someone had given you as a joke. It had a 3D reindeer on it and was covered in big red bobbly noses. Diane hated it and tried to get rid of it. You found it in the garbage bin and rescued it. Later that night you and she had a blazing row."

Matt was silent. His face was white and strained and he was so still Lily wondered if he'd stopped breathing.

"See," she said trying to prompt a response. "I couldn't possibly have known that, could I?"

"So," he said in such a low voice Lily had to lean forward to catch what he was saying. "So, Diane's put you up to this has she? I might have known! Not content with buggering off without a word, now she's come back for some kind of perverse revenge. Well, I'll thank you to get out of my house, and take that flea-ridden biscuit bag with you!"

Lily backed away from his anger. Then she said, after a quick glance at Seb: "I'm not in league with Diane, whoever she is, but I can also tell you that after she left, despite all the fuss you made about that sweater, you threw it away anyway. There's no way Diane could have known that, is there? Even if I were in league with her. Which I'm not."

That stopped him in his tracks. Clearly he couldn't work it out.

Neither could Lily. She looked at Seb and Caramel Girl. They both looked encouragingly back at her.

I'm getting all this from my Princess. She's getting it from inside Matt's head. She can communicate with anyone. Most Hounds can only communicate with their own Compeers.

Surely that would convince him. There was no other possible way she could have known he'd thrown that jumper away. Waiting for Matt's realisation that it was all true, everything she'd said about communicating with the dogs, Lily breathed more shallowly, afraid that the air would catch fire. The tension in the kitchen was so combustible. It was going to be such a relief to have someone else understand so completely what she was experiencing with Seb, and to get them on side in the quest to save the Realm. She could feel an involuntary smile start to curve the corners of her lips.

"Right. You just sit there. And don't try to get away or I'll have to restrain you. I don't suppose the police would be interested in an ex's idea of revenge, but I'm sure they'll want to know about a stalker who's been spying on me and going through my bins."

"What? What do you mean?" Lily's dream of having someone she could talk to about the whole Realm and talking-dog thing disappeared like a candle flame under a waterfall. The disappointment was so vast she nearly cried. Matt was talking into his telephone. She could see his mouth moving but couldn't hear what he was saying for the blood drumming in her head. Even Seb was confused.

Why's he gone all funny? What's he doing?

Gradually it dawned on Lily that it might be better for her health if she left Matt Lannings' house forthwith and she struggled to rise from her chair. As she did so, the doorbell rang. Whoever was out there kept their finger on it and the piercing shrilling continued. Maybe the bell was stuck. Lily glanced at Matt. Startlement appeared on his face, and he looked at his phone as if it had bitten him. He headed off to the front of the house and Lily sat down again. She would wait until he got back so she could leave with some dignity rather than slinking out of his back door.

But when he came back he was accompanied by several burly women and a couple of men in white coats. He seemed to be objecting to something, but they were ignoring him. He looked at Lily with an appeal on his face but she couldn't think what that was about and anyway, she'd had it with him. He was a Rude, Silly Git. But why was he mouthing 'sorry' at her now?

"I had no idea they'd turn up so fast," he said before he was escorted from the room by a couple of policemen with clipboards.

As soon as Matt was out of sight, hands clasped Lily's arms and heaved her upright.

"Oy! What are you doing?" she yelled as she found herself bundled towards the kitchen door, a brawny woman on either side of her, gripping her arms so hard they must be in danger of cutting off her circulation. Her legs weren't long enough and her feet barely touched the floor. One of the white-coated men was droning on. She couldn't hear it all. It sounded like one of those things you had to say by law as a kind of disclaimer. She picked out the phrases: "harm to yourself or others", "police", "public nuisance". What was worse was his breath – it was rank!

Think good thoughts!

"Think good thoughts? How the hell can I think good thoughts when I'm being manhandled by sumo wrestlers?" she shouted.

Be quiet you two! Lily stiffened with shock. She'd not had anyone in her head other than Seb. But this was Caramel Girl.

Looking towards the Hounds now she could see Caramel Girl standing so tensely her whole body quivered. Lily tried to listen, tried to look around, but her captors were crowding her too much. But then, a smell attacked her – a smell so strong it was physical. It pressed down on her lungs trying to close them. She tried to swing around, desperately searching for the source. Before she found it, wailing sirens approached, beating the air with their rising and falling screams. Snarls of rage fractured the evening. The noise paralysed her and she could make out no details of what she was seeing. She just knew it was the same malevolence as last night. Seb and Caramel Girl were lost in a maelstrom of darkness, a vortex of nothingness and madly whirling anger, teeth and blood.

Briefly she wondered if the Hounds were being deliberately distracted to prevent them from rescuing her.

Remembering Seb's exhortations Lily tried very hard to think of winning, to think of goodness and love, but she just felt like a useless idiot doing nothing to help her friends, and even more useless when the hands grasping her arms clamped down harder and she was propelled outside, past a confused-looking Matt still occupied by the policemen, and pushed into a waiting car.

"What the hell?" She struggled but a heavy pressure on her head as she was propelled into the police car let her know that she was under their control and might as well give up now. The handcuffs finally persuaded her to go still. Handcuffs? She'd been arrested? What on Earth for? For rootling around in Rude, Silly Git's bins? It was him who'd called the police and this was their answer?

"What's going on?" she demanded.

"Try not to worry," a policeman said.

She stared at him, a laugh almost making itself felt. "Try not to worry? You're kidding me. Right? Right? I'm manhandled into a car, restrained forcefully, handcuffed. Kidnapped. For no reason. And you're telling me not to worry…"

"We're going to get you the right treatment," he said in what he appeared to think were soothing tones. "Don't worry. We have an expert on his way to help with treatment."

"Treatment?" she yelled. "I don't need treatment!" The thought was so terrifying she found herself thrashing around, as if that would do any good. She stopped when she realised it might help give the impression that she actually ***needed*** restraining, and 'treatment'. She tried very hard to think of goodness and love. It didn't help her in the least but she did keep still. "Please tell me what's going on." She tried again.

"We know who you are, Lily. You really have nothing to worry about. Your parents sent us to look for you because they were so concerned about your welfare. And it did look like you were talking to a couple of mutts just then so everything they said about you coming off your meds seems to be correct, and we're taking you in for treatment before you deteriorate even more."

"Meds? I'm not on any meds. My parents? What have they got to do with anything? I thought Rude Git sent for you."

By the way the two in the back looked at each other when she said that she thought it would probably be best if she kept quiet.

Be calm. We will find you and rescue you. Think good thoughts.

And just like that she *was* calm. She wasn't so positive about thinking good stuff, though, considering all she wanted to do was kill a few people, including the patronising policeman, Rude Git, her parents, all Crules and any Betrayers that happened to be handy. But she tried.

Lily was transported to an enormous, gothic building which appeared to have no one else in it but them. There she was talked over, paperwork was filled out which seemed to need no input from her at all, and a few checks were made. Apparently her blood pressure was high. No, really!!!

She was absolutely seething, and somebody was going to be sorry before she was finished. She had never been treated with so little concern for her wishes and rights, and couldn't believe it when she was injected with something as well, without even being asked if she wanted it.

The trouble was that whatever was in the injection quickly had the effect of making her feel very, very far away from everything happening outside of her body. Inside her body, she could hear her breathing. It was intrusively loud. Her blood was loud, too, the way it rushed around the place. Her digestive system made some very peculiar and embarrassing noises. But when she tried to focus on anything outside of herself it was as if she was peering at it from the other end of a long cardboard tube and her field of vision was getting smaller and smaller. Her face felt as though it was a badly fitting mask, loosely attached to the front of her skull. It had never laughed; it didn't know how.

All the energy, everything that made her Lily Wilkins retreated to a very small part of her somewhere deep inside. By the time she'd been taken to some place called 'The Haven' which she thought might be a hospital, but wasn't sure, she was no longer convinced she was really who she thought she was despite the voice in her head telling her to: *Be calm. We will find you. Think good thoughts.* She had the idea the voice once meant a lot to her, but now it was more of an irritating buzz than a support.

* * * * *

In The Haven she quickly learnt that she could shuffle around her own room, down the corridor, around the sitting room and back to her room again if she counted every step. If she forgot to count she would come to a halt and someone would take her arm and lead her back to her room again where they would leave her sitting on the edge of her bed staring at the floor.

Before long, some compulsion would force her upright, she would start counting again and off she'd go. She knew she had to do it or she'd die. A very large, bristly edged, four-legged shadow by her side made her do it. It gave her no peace whenever she tried to sit down and die. It bullied her unmercifully. Even overnight, it made her get up and wander around much to the annoyance of the attendants who kept chivvying her back to bed. She was shattered the following morning but felt much more herself, and she knew that if not for the shadow she'd probably be dead. Thank you, she thought at it.

If she expected a reply she was disappointed. She couldn't make anything of the one word she thought she heard: *Sausages*. Sausages?

Time meant nothing in The Haven, but Lily thought it must be late morning the next day when her parents came to see her. She was shepherded into a little visitors' room with windows for walls, and her parents joined her in there. She looked at them and they looked at her. Attendants patrolled regularly past the room, staring in at them, presumably waiting for her to tear her mother's hair off, or try to disembowel her father with her nails.

As she could barely stop her head from lolling on her neck and her chin from constantly resting on her chest, she couldn't fathom how she was supposed to have the energy to attack anyone, but she wished she did have. She couldn't even see properly because her eyelids felt as though they had become dead things and constantly wanted to flop down and shut out the light to her eyes.

"I am so sorry," her mother said. "I had no idea this is what would happen. We just wanted you to be safe." But she couldn't hide her implacable disgust.

Why did her own mother hate her so much? Except Lily knew Carol wasn't her mother. Seb – the name came to her with a glorious clarity after she'd failed to grasp it all night – Seb had said this woman wasn't her mother, but Lily had chosen not to follow up on it. Surely, some part of her had always known Carol wasn't her mother. There was no doubt in her mind now.

Her father looked miserable, said nothing, and looked everywhere but at her. Lily wondered if he was her real father, but she thought he was. Wouldn't he know about the Realm, too? Was this thing genetic, or was she really a one-off? Except there was Rude Git, as well – he was supposed to be the same as her in that regard, but surely it wasn't just the two of them. Did it run in families? She knew she couldn't ask or it would be used as further evidence of the imbalance of her mind.

As long as she had Seb she'd be all right. At least she had him. Where was he, though? Now she was relatively undrugged why wasn't he in her mind?

Guarded.

Oh. That must mean there were Crules about. She wouldn't even recognise them so she couldn't be much help on that score. She told Seb to shut up forthwith, and stop broadcasting! There was no answer, not even a reassuring *Heck!* or *Sausages!* She had never felt so alone.

Chapter Six

Matt couldn't believe it when the police turned up so fast. He'd never complain about paying council tax again. What a great service! One minute he had a stalker in his house, the next she had been taken away by the local police service seconds after he'd called them.

He had felt badly at the time. Lily had looked so shocked, and small, and so alone. He was sorry for her. Poor thing, to actually believe she could communicate with her dog and rely on him to protect her. He shook his head marvelling at her delusions. There was nothing quite as unknown as the workings of the human brain. But everyone has to draw the line somewhere; it was all very well feeling sympathy for a fellow human being in trouble, but to find that she'd been conspiring with Diane to further his torment, and then to go through his bins as well... A man has to take a stand.

Why did he feel so very badly about it, then?

Feeling eyes upon him he turned to find Amber staring at him. She radiated sorrow and he rushed over and hugged her. She didn't relax into him, though, like she normally did and he wondered if having that mob coming in like that had upset her. They had been pretty brusque and heavy-handed. The thought made him squirm with discomfort and he hugged Amber harder, but intense guilt soon followed. Fancy having a young girl treated like that just because she'd been rootling through his bins. It might have sounded sinister at the time, but on reflection it surely wasn't such a crime that she should have been taken away quite like that. And where was that other pesky dog? It had been sitting here. It had got a bit agitated when Lily was taken away and at one point he'd lost sight of both dogs but Amber was here now, so where was the other one?

He made himself a big breakfast. He felt the need after the last couple of days. But once it was cooked he merely stared at it, poking the yolk until it ruptured and stabbing the bacon as though it needed killing. It was no good – he had to find out what had happened to the dog. Who would look after it while Lily was away? He couldn't think of it roaming the streets, starving and mystified at suddenly having no home.

Amber was eager to accompany him as he left the house. He didn't take the car as it was only a few streets to Lily's place. He'd overheard her address being read out when the police and medical personnel had come to identify Lily before taking her away. Matt took a spare lead with him. Maybe the dog had gone back to Lily's house, in which case he would bring him back to stay with him and Amber until Lily was home again. That was the simplest way of dealing with the problem.

As he approached Lily's house expecting to find the door shut and locked he was surprised to see it standing open. He stopped, unsure of what to do. There was no sign of the dog. A woman appeared in the doorway carrying a box. It looked like she'd raided the fridge. What on Earth? Matt, feeling uncomfortable because this whole thing had nothing to do with him, approached her.

"Can I ask what's happening about Lily, please? And her dog?"

"She's in The Haven. I've no idea about any dog."

"Are you a neighbour, or family, maybe?" The woman turned away without answering. A man came out carrying a box of what looked like greeting cards. He seemed uncomfortable and wouldn't look directly at Matt. "We're her parents," he said. "My wife is…"

"*You* might be her parent. *I'm* not!" And the woman stomped off, threw the box into the back of a car, got in the front passenger seat, and slammed the door.

The man flushed. "Are you a friend?" he asked Matt. "We did what we thought best. She is unwell." He glanced at the car. "Lily, that is. It's Lily who is unwell. We thought it best she got some treatment before she became even worse." He shifted from foot to foot.

Matt looked pointedly at the box in his arms.

"I'm trying to fulfil the orders she's already got," Lily's father said. "I'll shut down her online stores for the time being. Better that than she gets orders in and can't fill them and get a bad name after all her hard work building the business. That's what these are. Cards for orders." He trailed off uncertainly.

Matt didn't know why Lily's father was still talking to him. He didn't have to explain anything to him. It was as if he wanted to say something else, but didn't know how.

After more shiftiness he suddenly hissed: "Please visit her." Lily's father flicked his gaze in his wife's direction and back to Matt. "Lily seems so alone, and my wife won't let me go in to see her again."

"It was you who got her put in hospital?" Matt said, a feeling of such enormous relief flooding him that he would have promised anything out of sheer gratitude that Lily's incarceration wasn't down to him after all. "Of course I'll visit her. I'd like to be able to tell her that her dog is safe, too. Do you know where he is?"

Again the furtive look towards his wife. "I don't know anything about a dog," Lily's father said, avoiding Matt's gaze, and shuffled off down the path.

Matt watched them drive away. If he felt sorry for Lily before, he felt even more so now. With parents like that – anyone would start talking to their dog!

He and Amber walked back to his house. With every step he wondered if he should be getting involved. He was worried about the dog, but did he really want to have anything more to do with Lily Wilkins? She was interfering, thoroughly irritating, in some kind of conspiracy scheme with his ex-fiancée, and she talked to her dog. Trouble was, he'd promised her father he'd visit his daughter, now. He sighed and Amber butted his thigh with her head. He fondled her ears and felt better. Having a dog was definitely good for his health.

Yes, he would visit Lily because he'd promised he would, and because he was very lucky and she obviously wasn't. He could at least let her know things were all right with her dog if only he could find him first, and reassure her that although he didn't believe that dogs and humans could talk to each other, he had no problem with people who **believed** they could. He was a scientist and being a scientist didn't mean **not** believing in things he couldn't see. It meant believing that anything was possible until it was proved otherwise. And no one had ever actually proved that humans and dogs couldn't speak to each other.

Not that he'd be happy to stand on a soap box with a megaphone and tell the world that, but if it would make Lily feel better he was happy to say it to her given that she appeared to have no one else to back her up.

This was what made him feel bad. That someone, anyone, could have no one prepared to support them. After witnessing the spectacle of her parents abandoning her so completely – and what a wimp her father was! – he couldn't in all conscience walk away himself.

Matt had visited The Haven once before when a colleague with no family of his own had become ill after a horribly stressful year. Matt wasn't too sure quite what type of institution it was. It didn't seem to fit the bill of an average hospital, and he thought it must be privately run. Still, it seemed efficient and clean enough, not that he knew that much about these things. However, the memory of being shut in between the two outer doors, even though for a very short time, filled him with apprehension. It was alarming to find out how easily he could be trapped somewhere he'd gone voluntarily.

Knowing the drill after being let through the outer door, he signed himself in very quickly and turned to the second door sighing with relief when he heard the 'click' that signified it had been unlocked and he was able to walk through. He didn't mind being shut into the main body of the hospital nearly as much as being shut into that little bit in between the doors.

What was worse was that he'd lied in the signing-in book. As soon as the nurse behind the desk had said it was only close relatives allowed in he changed his surname for Lily's. Surely that wasn't such a bad lie… He looked around as if waiting for the wrath of gods to fall on him and squash him flat. It didn't. If he was really pushed he'd say he was her brother. If he was lucky no one would question it and he wouldn't have to say it. And if he didn't have to say it out loud then it wasn't really lying was it?

Waiting in one of the little visiting rooms that had windows for walls he wondered what he was going to say to her. They barely knew each other and had only met on unfortunate occasions. What was he doing here? He leapt to his feet and paced the room. Maybe he should leave before the nurse who'd gone to find her came back. Why did he think Lily would want to see him anyway? He couldn't even tell her about her dog, having failed to find him. He'd made an awful mistake. He must leave!

But he couldn't just disappear, and he couldn't go in case the nurse had told Lily he was here, and maybe she did want to see him, and then she'd get to the visiting room and he wouldn't be there and then he'd be just another person who'd let her down.

Indecision kept him immobile so when the door opened and Lily stood there leaning heavily on the handle as though it was the only thing keeping her upright, they gazed at each other for a long time before Lily let go of the handle and stumbled towards him, falling into his arms as though she could stand no longer. He staggered backwards until the wall prevented him going any further, and simply held her.

Eventually, she pulled away and they both sat down as though the touching and hugging thing had never happened. Matt tried hard to keep his face expressionless, but he felt ill looking at Lily. She looked dreadful – unkempt and desperate. He thought she must be heavily drugged. Her eyes rolled a bit and keeping them open appeared to be a heavy chore, while her head wanted to sink forward to rest her chin on her chest. She struggled to keep it upright.

Barely containing his remorse at seeing this vibrant character brought so low Matt jumped up. "Let's go outside into the garden and get some fresh air." He'd seen the garden on his way through the enormous grounds the hospital stood in. He held out his hand to Lily who, after staring at it for a long time, took it and allowed herself to be pulled to her feet.

"It's your fault I'm here," she slurred. Nevertheless, she allowed him to lead her out of the visiting room, through a communal tea-making area, through a sitting room full of people watching a pig in a purple-feathered hat on a huge television screen, and out through French windows to a large and pleasant area with a crazy-paving patio covered in cigarette ends, and a generous expanse of grass with wooden benches dotted about.

Matt really wanted to tell Lily that it wasn't him who had got her put in here, but he was worried the effort of understanding it was her parents' doing might be too much for her in her present state.

They strolled to the end of the garden away from the congregated smokers, and the groups of people sitting on the grass. He thought it was a bit cold to be sitting on the ground, but each to their own. Lily's arm remained through his as though they often walked together arm-in-arm to view the flowers and make small talk about the weather, not that the small talk was flowing at all…

It was nice that the clinic, or whatever this place was, had such a large garden. It wasn't too exciting, landscaping-wise, but it had a few weed-free flower beds and a lot of open area for people to get away by themselves if they wanted. The fence around it, although solid, wasn't very high. He wondered if people escaped over that fence. He also wondered if they broke *in* over that fence. And, indeed, if some broke out and then broke back in again if they wanted a break from the place. He was puzzled as to the reasoning behind the height of that fence. It was neither one thing nor another – it couldn't prevent anyone from getting in or out, but yet it wasn't a decorative feature, being of a very sturdy, overlap larch construction.

Lily, he knew, in her usual limber state, rather than her present comatose one, would have no difficulty leaping over it. Glancing to his right he could see a similar building with an outside bit but around that was a fence that went forever skyward and then had a ceiling bit of fence too – no chance of breaking out of there. Sympathy for the people locked in there shivered through him. How unfortunate to have one's chemical levels so out of whack that one should end up in there. *If* that was why they were there. He was beginning to wonder if this place wasn't used just to dump 'inconvenient' people too. After all, Lily was hardly a menace to society, or to herself. Why was she in here at all? Why had her parents really had her incarcerated? It couldn't possibly have been just because she talked to her dog. That was too ridiculous!

Even greater puzzlement bloomed within him as he surveyed the patch of grass he'd brought them to. What had prompted him to come outside at all, let alone come to this corner of the garden which had no bench to sit on or even any flowers to look at apart from a small clump of something vaguely pinky-greeny. He looked around and considered sitting on the grass, but really, it did look horribly damp. Not that he was too worried, but he didn't want Lily getting a chill as well as being drugged up to the eyeballs and appearing to have no one who gave a monkey's about her.

A movement caught his eye and for the first time he noticed Lily looking interested rather than blank. He stared in the same direction. As he did so, he spotted what looked like a fat tuft of hair moving along the top of the fence. For a moment he could make no sense of it, but then a sinking feeling in his gut convinced him he was seeing the tip of the tail of a very large dog. Sure enough, a furry, grinning face suddenly appeared and disappeared, appeared and disappeared, as the very large dog he'd previously been so worried about bounced up and down on the other side of the fence.

Doom-laden pangs in his stomach convinced Matt that he knew what he was expected to do. He couldn't pin down just who was doing the expecting. There was only him, Lily and that mangy mutt present. How was it possible for him to feel so obliged, so compelled, to help Lily escape? He couldn't do it! He was an upright, respectable, law-abiding citizen and Lily had been incarcerated according to the due processes of law. He would *not* break the law just because some dog was somehow making him feel he should. He resisted with all his strength.

So much for worrying about that mutt! To think he'd been concerned about him feeling all neglected and unloved and roaming the streets, starving and not knowing why he'd suddenly lost his home. And here he was, that mutt, engaged in criminal activities! At the same time, Matt was conscious of the ludicrous nature of his internal rant. How could he possibly believe the impulse to help Lily to escape had anything to do with a dog?

All the time Matt's internal battle raged on, the mutt's face kept appearing, disappearing, appearing, disappearing as he bounded up and down on the other side of the fence.

Lily broke away from Matt and stumbled towards the dog. Reaching the fence she leaned against it as if all her energy had been used up in those few steps. Matt watched as she fumbled her hands up the wooden slats and pressed them flat against the wood as if she could feel through it to the warmth of the body on the other side.

Undecided, Matt stood for a moment. But then he saw the silvery tracing of tears as they rolled down her face and without realising what he was about he'd crossed the short distance, lifted her bodily in his arms and held her high enough that she was able to get her feet and legs over the fence. She struggled, he let her go, and she disappeared from view. Matt stared at the wood in front of his face and wondered what the hell he'd just done.

"Oy! You!"

Matt swung around to see some hefty attendants bearing down on him. A crowd of other inmates had gathered at the top of the garden as if witnessing a drama.

This was ridiculous. All he'd done was help her do something she could have easily done herself if she hadn't been drugged into immobility.

But they didn't look pretty, the attendants advancing on him. They'd gone into a crouch as if they were cornering a dangerous beast. If they carried tridents and big nets he wouldn't have been surprised. They meant business.

Backing up as far as he could, his hands held in front of him, palms out defensively, he said, "Now come on. There's no need to approach me like this. I'm no danger to anyone."

"Of course you are. For a start, you signed in as her brother. You're not her brother. She doesn't have a brother. So who the hell are you? Not to mention you've just helped a patient to escape. A very ill patient. Heaven knows what will happen to her out there." The very broad, very muscular nurse jerked her head to indicate the wide world beyond the garden fence. Matt couldn't help but notice that Nurse Muscular's hands were ***enormous***!

"She could easily have got out by herself," he said, heavy misgivings in his heart. He had a dire feeling that he wasn't going to get away with this like he really felt he should. All his life he had expected to be able to reason his way out of sticky situations. Suddenly, he knew his life was no longer something ruled by reason and logic.

The impulse to run like hell was overwhelming, but he couldn't make himself believe that these people actually meant to restrain him, maybe lock him up, maybe drug him insensible. He was a law-abiding, tax-paying, boring vet who never parked in disabled spaces. Why would they want to do that to *him*?

Playing for time he said, "If you're that worried about people getting out, why is the fence so low?"

"If it's too high, it's intimidating for the patients," Nurse Muscular said with a remarkably straight face despite the accompaniment of a snort of surprised laughter from one of her colleagues, whose hands Matt just happened to notice were also huge. And then Matt spotted the third nurse and that guy had a syringe in his hand and he was doing something with it that looked remarkably like he was preparing to use it after he'd finished waving it around in a menacing fashion. That did it.

Much to Nurse Muscular's surprise, Matt propelled himself forward, collided off her, did a sudden turnabout and ran full tilt at the fence. He vaulted over it, landing hard but upright, still maintaining a foothold on the ground. He ran after the crazily bouncing dogs ahead of him. He could see Amber. What was she doing here?

He couldn't see Lily until he realised she was draped over her mutt's back. Logically, he couldn't see how that dog could be carrying her, but logic was beginning to seem so outmoded in his current Lily-influenced life that he didn't question it for too long.

He simply ran like hell.

As he fled the scene of his crime, a strange feeling overtook him, lifting him higher from the earth, making him move faster; the wind rushed into his face and parted to let him through, combing his hair on its way. After a moment he realised the strange feeling was exultation. He was happy. He laughed aloud.

Could he remember the last time he'd been consciously happy? No, he couldn't. This seemed like the most inappropriate time to feel like this, but he was going to revel in it while he could. He knew from bitter experience that it wouldn't last.

Impossibly, he ran even faster. It was a joy for him to be part of his own body. He hadn't run just for the sake of it for years. He'd been a top runner back in a previous life when he was carefree. Maybe he'd take it up again.

When they reached the street he lived in he came back to reality with a groan. Police cars were stationed at each end of the road. He dived for cover behind a badly parked camper van and peered out. He could see from here there was a barricade around his front door, and no doubt around the back, too. A lot of people appeared to be waiting for him to come home. Withstanding the compulsion to turn up his collar and slink off, he ducked down again and tried to decide what to do. Looking around, he saw the dogs behind him, Lily still draped over one of them. She lifted her head as he watched and muttered: "Are we home yet?"

No one answered her.

Matt turned back to the sight in front of him. It would seem that he, a respectable vet, couldn't get into his own home. Not without being arrested. How had they got here so quickly? How could they have known it was him at The Haven? He'd not used his real name. Unless there really **was** this network of Crules, whatever they were, and… No! He wasn't going down that ludicrous path. This must be a mistake. They couldn't be here to arrest him. No one could have worked out it was him at The Haven. They must be here for a different reason. That was all right, then.

As he marched out of hiding, he heard Lily's soft wail: "Noooo…" and he felt a tugging in his mind urging him to stay put, but he kept going. He lived in a civilised country. These conspiracy theories were products of a fevered brain like Lily's. He refused to pander to them. Absolutely refused!

As he approached his own home he realised that some of the waiting people had big cameras resting on their shoulders. This was the local news team, maybe? What on Earth for? Looking properly now he could see others wearing thick protective vests and holding shields. He looked over his shoulder. They couldn't possibly be waiting for him. At the sound of the police helicopter getting nearer he realised that someone must have escaped the local jail. There was no other answer. Unfortunately for him they must have taken refuge in his garden.

He was close enough now to see the police nearest his front door had a battering ram. A battering ram! That stopped him. A battering ram!?! Then, with utter horror, he realised that the big white vehicle that looked like a fire engine only not in red, must be a water cannon. A water cannon!!! Since when did they even *have* water cannon in this country?

A shout went up and the crowd surged towards him. The escaped criminal must have got behind him. He turned to look and someone grabbed his arm and shouted: "Got him! I've got him!" and yanked hard. Nearly falling, Matt managed to keep his footing only by pulling against the guy who was still triumphantly yelling that he'd caught the villain. He smelled of peppermints and sweat and wore a helmet complete with protective visor as though Matt was about to spray him with acid.

There must have been a major mistake made, a terrible confusion. Why was he being treated like an escaped and violent desperado? There was no way there had been time for The Haven to work out who he was and get here before him.

Was there a conspiracy? Was Lily right? No! It was too ridiculous, dammit!

But Helmet-guy grabbed him again and the rest of the mob were fast surrounding him. Kicking out, Matt's foot connected with Helmet-guy's shin. He let go of Matt's arm and Matt was off. He ran for his life for the second time in an hour, more confused than he'd ever been. He was pleased he managed to keep enough reason to run in the opposite direction to where the dogs and Lily were though, rather than take the crowd their way.

He wasn't worried about being caught. He'd been a top runner when at school and at university. It really was beginning to look like it was a good thing for him to take up again. He would start practising forthwith!

Matt was petrified that his life had disintegrated into something that he had to keep running away from. And it was all that Lily Wilkins's fault!

Chapter Seven

Gradually, the darkness in her mind weakened, the light strengthened, and Lily opened her eyes to stare at a ceiling she'd never seen before. Fear jolted through her; she kicked away the duvet and jack-knifed to a sitting position, surprising a startled bark from Seb who threw himself off the bed and pretended he'd never been on it. Lily eyed him suspiciously.

Don't know why you're looking at me like that...

"Hmphh!"

Time for breakfast.

"It's always time for breakfast as far as you're concerned."

What's wrong with breakfast?

"Nothing. At breakfast-time. But it must be at least evening if not night-time by now." Lily stared around her. Nothing looked familiar. A strange churning started up in her stomach as fleeting pictures of the near past came back to her. "Where are we?" she demanded.

It's morning. Sunday morning. We're staying at a friend's house. We couldn't go back to yours after Matt got you out of the big doghouse. Yours is where they'll look for you first.

Lily chose to ignore the frightening reality of what he'd said and picked instead on another question. "What friend? This doesn't look familiar to me at all." She looked around again to check. Nope. Not familiar at all. And anyway, if it was a friend of hers she didn't want to bring all that trouble down on them. They would have to leave straightaway.

*Not **your** friend.* **My** *friend.*

"You have friends?"

Why would I not have friends? He sounded decidedly huffy which didn't sit well on his whiskery face. Lily worked hard not to laugh.

"How can you have friends **here,** I mean? You've never been in the Human Territories before." She thought that was perfectly reasonable logic.

Maybe not friends exactly, but dogs who are for the cause, dogs who dream of the Realm. We're in Barker and Ruby's house. They will become names to conjure with, honorary members of the Realm. They regularly stand out in their garden and bark and howl and spread the word. Just like in their favourite puphood book, the One Hundred and Three Tailwaggers in which they outwit the Crule who wants all the pups so she can make a set of hand luggage out of their skins.

"Uh.... I think you'll find it's one hundred and one..."

Oh, piffle and waffle! One hundred and one, one hundred and three – what's the difference?

"Uh... two..."

Exactly! Not much difference. Yeah, so, Barker and Ruby have dreamed of saving the Realm their whole lives. And now they are. Well, a bit of it. Sort-of.

"What about their humans?"

They're under the paw. No worries there.

Lily couldn't begin to imagine how any humans would be happy to countenance giving shelter to a bunch of fugitives they didn't know, some of them four-legged, running from the law, the health authorities, and the Crules as well. Wouldn't their presence put Barker and Ruby and their humans in danger?

They're not here. This is one of our safe houses in the Human Territories. Barker and Ruby and their humans have gone away for a week to the Lake District.

"Oh, I see. Thank goodness for that. I was wondering what to say when I bumped into them in their kitchen. Maybe: *'Thank you so much for letting us stay in your spare room. Sorry my dog got on the bed and left lots of fur lying around and a bit of an aroma. We're escaping from the police, medical personnel – oh, and a load of Crules. It's very kind of you to let us raid your larder while we're here.'* Would that fit the bill?"

You know, sarcasm needs to be a little more subtle for full effect. Seb's tone was full of stuffiness.

"So, how are we here? And how is this safe for them?"

Barker and Ruby left messages on the howling vine so we'd know where the keys are, and as long as you make sure that anything you eat looks like a dog's been at it, they've offered to take the blame for any food we consume. So their humans will never know we were here and the Crules won't be interested in them even if they do find us here. But they won't. They can sense us when we broadcast, but there is a permanent guard around this house. That's why it's one of our safe houses. Barker and Ruby have spent years thinking Human Territories' dog thoughts so the house is surrounded by them which prevents detection of our kind of communication. They've also spent a lot of time educating their humans in the kind of nosh they should get when they go shopping so that if we should ever need to use their home for shelter there would be plenty of sausages. And pizza.

"So how do we make baking a pizza in the oven look like our congenial hosts Barker and Ruby have done it? If they're away with their humans on holiday, how can they be here at the same time eating all the pizzas and sausages?"

You can't bake them! You'll have to eat them raw.

"Uh. I think I might give it a miss..."

Don't say you weren't offered a feast!

"I won't. Are there any biscuits? Or cake? Cake's fine."

Your diet is so unhealthy!

"No cake?"

Nope.
"Oh, no!"
Just kidding.

On further investigation of the house, Lily was startled to find Matt in the kitchen, Caramel Girl under the table. Matt, a steaming mug of coffee at his elbow, doodled on paper with a slightly chewed pencil. As Lily entered he jumped to his feet. "Coffee?" He switched on the kettle without waiting for a reply and set about collecting cafetière, ground coffee, and mug.

"Thanks. That would be great. What are you doing here?"

"I can't go home. I've helped an unstable patient escape from hospital; in doing so I apparently assaulted several members of the medical staff, and now I'm wanted for questioning."

"An unstable patient? Are you referring to me?"

"Do you still insist that you can talk to the animals?"

Lily slumped into a chair. Was she unstable? Really?

Of course you're not!

"I'm the only one who can '*hear*' you, Seb. How do I know I'm not unstable?"

Do I look unstable?

Lily stared into Seb's face. He looked intelligent enough. He definitely had taken up some kind of lodging in her head. But did that mean she and he could actually communicate? In real words?

Yes! I've demonstrated this to you repeatedly. I'm not doing it again. Got any sausages?

"Wait a minute," she said, turning back to Matt. "If you don't believe in it, why are you here? Why did you rescue me from the hospital?"

"I didn't rescue you from the hospital. I admit I gave you a leg up over the fence, but the moving force, as it were, was your dog. You could just as well have got over that fence by yourself. If you'd been awake enough. As for being here – I just followed the crowd when I discovered I couldn't go home. This is where Seb brought you. Amber came too. I just followed. I can't go home. I can't go back to my work. Somehow, since you came into my life, it's no longer the life I used to have."

Oddly, he didn't seem all that upset about it. He was matter-of-fact even though his words announced a catastrophic change.

Maybe he doesn't feel anything any more. Maybe he can't. Awww... Seb wandered over to Matt and slurped at his arm where his sleeve was rolled up. Matt wasn't at all grateful and snatched his slobbered-limb away. "Aarghh! Don't do that. I don't want dog gob all over me!"

"He was sympathising with you!" Lily yelled and running over to Seb she dropped to her knees and gave him a hug.

No worries. I've survived worse rejection than this. Seb's tone was stoic, but resigned. *We're not doing very well with him are we? How can we convince him before it's too late?*

"Before it's too late?"

We don't have much time left for the Great Reconciliation to take place. It has to happen before next Wednesday which is when the Path opens again. After that, it doesn't open again for ages and by then it's possible there'll be no Betrayer to reconcile with.

"The Path? No, never mind about the Path – why might there be no Betrayer by then?"

"She might have died, or been killed, or she might get lost in the Void next Wednesday when the Path opens. Or, it's even possible that the Greatly Betrayed might have perished by then so there'd be no one to reconcile with."

"I'm not sure all the drugs are out of my system," Lily muttered, her head weaving with all these new ideas about Paths and Voids and perishing. "Where's my coffee?"

Matt pushed a mug into her hand. He got some things right. The coffee was exactly what she needed. Nice and strong, too.

"When you've had that and the dogs had some breakfast – by the way – your dog is always starving – has he been wormed recently?"

"Have you been wormed recently?" Lily asked Seb, just managing not to laugh.

He merely showed his teeth and laid his head back down on his paws. Caramel Girl licked his ear in sympathy. Poor Seb, trying so hard in such an ungrateful world.

"When you've quite finished talking to the dog, I think we need to check out our homes. I'd have thought that after the usual Saturday night chaos in the city centre, the police won't be interested in us. Why would they be? I'll clear up here and we can get going."

One of the things Lily had noticed about Rude Git was that he often didn't require anyone to have a conversation with. He just made announcements and no one needed to reply. So she didn't. She savoured her coffee and watched him make the kitchen look like no one had ever been in it. Then he disappeared upstairs presumably to do the same thing.

"Thank you, Barker and Ruby," she said as they left through the back door of the house.

"Who are you talking to now?" Matt said. "I don't know whose house this is, but I'm only thankful we had it to shelter in so I'm not going to ask. Forget I asked."

Skulking around the streets they got to Lily's house with no untoward incidents. The house opposite hers had a handy hedge onto the road and lying pressed up against Seb's side behind that hedge Lily could clearly see her parents being busy with her stuff. What were they were doing with it? Why were they were doing anything at all with it?

On reflection, as they'd had her locked up in The Haven for being inconvenient, it was anybody's guess what they were up to. It was obvious, however, that her house was not going to be a refuge for her. Possibly not ever again. She leaned into Seb, only just preventing herself from putting her arms around his neck by the withering look he gave her and the whisper of a growl in her mind. Nope. She wasn't that feeble!

Unexpectedly, the door behind them squealed open and a voice said: "Lily? Is that you, dear? Your mother's looking for you."

Seb and Lily jumped to their feet and ran. A shout ripped the air, the sound of car doors slamming and an engine revving encouraged in them extra speed as they raced up the street and around the corner. They dived into someone else's garden just in time to peer out and see Lily's parents screeching past in their car.

"How lovely to see you," someone said. Turning, Lily saw an elderly man, his trowel poised in mid-air. He was on his knees in a pair of those kneeling pads people use when they're gardening. "You're always welcome to drop in, but it would be nice if you could get off my crocuses. They're crying out to me to rescue them from your weight. I'll get in some Battenberg cake for next time you call. Bye now." And he turned back to his weeding.

"Okay," Lily whispered somewhat dazedly, although if she reckoned she could talk to dogs why couldn't crocuses talk to this man? She and Seb set off to scout out Matt's house instead, seeing as hers would be of no use to them in the foreseeable future.

They found Matt and Caramel Girl already there, having gained access through his back garden. The whole street was quiet again as if the hefty police presence yesterday had never happened.

"Come in, come in!" he said, waving them through the conservatory and into the kitchen. "We need to plan something to get our normal lives back. Although how we can get our normal lives back when they've gone so strangely abnormal I don't really know."

We've got to get him to believe. Time's running out! You must try again. How about a bit of history? You both need to know it.

Lily checked out Matt's face. It was more than ordinarily grim and she quailed from the thought of trying to get him to believe about talking dogs and stuff again. It was beyond her. She sat down and rested her head on her arms. She didn't want to see that disbelieving face any more.

Come on! You've got to save the Realm! You're the One Who Knows! It's the One Who Knows who effects our salvation. You've got a job to do. Pull yourself together!

Seb's will was inexorable. Lily sat up and faced Matt. "Let's make a big cafetière of coffee. I have a feeling this is going to be a long day."

He said nothing, but he did put the kettle on, then he leaned against the side with his arms crossed, a far-from-receptive expression on his face, and waited.

"Well, um… Well, the only way to do this is for me to tell you the history of this situation. But I don't know it either. It's all coming from Seb. So I'll just tell it to you as it comes to me."

She paused, but there was no response from Matt.

"Okay, then. It's like this." Seb started to recite his story as though he'd done it many times before. Lily said his words aloud for him: "Caramel Girl – Amber – and I are Hounds. We live in the Realm. We used to share the Realm with our Compeers, humans with whom we could communicate. But the Great Betrayer, when looking for a mate in the Human Territories, brought back a Crule and would not bring herself to believe that was what she'd done. So he, this Crule, caused havoc in the Realm. He addicted some Hounds and some Compeers to the drug, clawkle, and he claimed large tracts of land to dig in for worthless stones and metals. And our Compeers found they could not resist his promises and so we all fought each other. We had to get this evil from our land and so the Great Betrayer Wars came about. They went on too long and too much damage was done. In the end we threw all the Compeers out."

Lily hesitated because Matt had got up and walked around her. Then he sat down again. "What?" she asked.

"Just checking to see if Seb has his paw up your back and is pulling your strings."

"You're very rude. You're a Rude Git."

Matt laughed and poured them both coffee.

Lily glanced at Seb and he started again, his voice low: "This is where the actions of my grandsire caused our family to live in shame forever. He couldn't dispose of his Compeer the way he should have. Instead of flinging her into the Void of Nothingness he let her escape. Because she was in pup he got soft, and because of him the Realm might die. His Compeer was the Great Betrayer who had brought the Crule to the Realm."

Poor Seb. Lily could see he was having to force himself to tell the tale, but he continued anyway.

"After my grandsire failed in his duty to the Realm, that Crule killed him. He only succeeded because my grandsire knew he'd failed his queen, and he wanted to die. Unfortunately, his mate, my grandam, was already in pup with my mother so our line still continues and we have to live with this shame til our line either dies out or the world ends." Seb went quiet and bowed his head.

"Right, so in this story different species mate, do they? A Compeer and a Crule?"

"Not different species. They are both humans, but one is good and the other evil. Well, that used to be the case. Now we have good *and* bad in the descendants of the Compeers, unfortunately."

"Where are the descendants?" Matt asked.

"They're here," Lily said. "All Compeers were thrown out of the Realm, so any of the remaining original Compeers and all descendants are here in the Human Territories, although very, very secret for the sake of self-preservation. Some don't even know themselves what they are."

To be fair to Matt, now they'd got this far into the story he did appear to be giving it serious thought. Lily felt a surge of hope.

Seb started up again and Lily pressed on: "Compeers here were divided between those who wanted to get back to the Realm and hung onto their Realm ideals, and those who wanted revenge for being thrown out. Crules and Crules-in-training want to kill all Compeers because if they ever get the chance to get back into the Realm it will be easier for them to overcome the Hounds alone, because without their Compeers Hounds are lesser. To be complete and function properly Hounds need their Compeers. And the same goes for Compeers – they are better off with their Hounds than alone. It's like a symbiotic relationship." Lily glanced at Matt. "Do you know what a symbiotic…"

"Of course I do!"

Eek. "Okay, okay. Just checking. Anyway, yeah, so we have to have the Great Reconciliation take place before the Path of Valediction opens on Wednesday and we have to go home."

"The Path of Valediction," Matt murmured and rolled his eyes.

Lily restrained herself and ploughed on: "Caramel Girl has arrived here to be with you. You are a descendant of a Compeer, only your family was very, very successful at guarding yourselves so you don't know it and you don't feel it, yet. Lily's family was also successful, but not quite so much which is why Lily left home as soon as she could and since then she's been totally confused about quite what she is, which made it easier to get her to realise that she is, in fact, a Compeer."

Matt actually snorted.

"This explains why you're a vet. You were drawn to animals and I bet most of your patients are dogs," Lily said. She had decided the best thing to do was ignore him at least until she'd got all the information out that Seb was flooding into her head. "Compeers and their descendants can't help it – they find themselves working with animals one way or another, or spend all their spare time doing so. They might become vets, or zoo keepers; they might volunteer to work on the city farm."

Seb got up to lap at the water bowl and Lily said: "It all fits. My father lectures at the university on zoology. Unfortunately, he might have used dogs for research purposes when he started even if not now because the law's changed and he's not allowed to. He was brought up in a guarded family, as I was, only he didn't manage to get away from them." She scrubbed at her face until it hurt, trying not to think of all those dogs used for experimentation. "And you're a vet," she said to Matt. "You didn't become a vet for no reason."

"I became a vet because I wanted to become a vet. I can't see the need for there to be any other deeper or more significant reason," he said, apparently struggling – and failing – to keep the scorn from his voice.

Lily stared at him. He wasn't going to believe any of this in a million years. She was so tired and so fed up with it all. Why did they need him anyway?

"Can't we do without him?" she asked Seb.

No, we can't.

She dropped her head onto her arms and shut her eyes.

Chapter Eight

Matt couldn't believe he was still sitting here listening to this drivel. He must be more drained than he thought. He'd had barely any sleep last night worrying about the state Lily was in. It bothered him that she'd been drugged so easily by the so-called authorities for no reason other than she talked to dogs. Also, it didn't suit him to stay in someone else's house when they weren't even there and he didn't know them. But since meeting Lily he was doing all kinds of things he'd never have dreamt of doing only a few days ago.

He looked at Caramel Girl – Amber! Her name was Amber! Surely that couldn't be *pity* in her gaze. She was a dog for Pete's sake! Just a dog! He yelped as a sharp pain blossomed in his ankle and travelled up his leg. He knew what it was. "Stop that dog from biting me!" he snapped, pulling his leg back and furiously rubbing the offended spot. He absolutely was not going to look at that great black hairy rug Lily called a dog. He swung both his legs onto the sofa just in case Seb was thinking of biting him again.

Or nip. To be fair. They were nips, not bites. If that animal really wanted to bite him he thought it likely he wouldn't escape just by removing his limbs from its proximity. He probably wouldn't *have* any limbs...

"Take no notice," Lily said airily, raising her head from her arms and waving her hand around as though being bitten by a Hound the size of a small horse was a mere gnat's kiss. "He is a very opinionated dog. The point is – what line are your parents in? Actually, I know nothing about you – what are your parents?"

"Dead. That's what," he growled. "Dead." He was gratified to see the blush that suffused her face and the discomfort that accompanied it. He was surprised the pleasure didn't last long and was almost immediately followed by remorse. "Sorry," he said. "Sorry, I shouldn't have said it like that. They've been dead for a few years. They died by suicide shortly after I graduated. It was as if they hung on long enough to get me that far, and then I didn't need them any more. The coroner brought in a verdict of accidental death, but I know it was no accident."

He looked up and the horror was back on Lily's face. He hastened on: "But it's all right. I'm a big boy now. Their lives – they could do what they wanted with them and at least they'd fulfilled their obligations to their child, or at least they thought they had. And there's no way of me knowing what they had to live with so I can't judge. And before you ask, they had nothing to do with dogs."

There, that would spike Lily's guns. "My father was campaign manager for a charity, and my mother was a counsellor…" His voice faltered and trailed off. Suddenly he wanted to go for a very long holiday to the Outer Hebrides. How very odd that after his entire life thinking of his parents' occupations in one way, now out of the blue he was thinking of them in another…

"What did they do exactly?" Lily asked. "What was the charity your father worked for? What kind of counsellor was your mother?"

"Oh, come on," Matt said. "You can make anything look like it's something to do with animals. I mean, if my father had been a baker, for instance, I have no doubt you'd try to convince me that he was baking treats for dogs that helped them get a good night's sleep, or if he'd been a dentist you'd say it was because he no doubt filled dogs' teeth in his spare time."

"Now you're being silly," Lily said as though he were a small child needing scolding.

"*I'm* being silly. *Me*. *I'm* the one being silly!" He laughed but abruptly stopped. It had sounded, even to his own ears, a tad hysterical.

Lily crossed her arms and tilted her head sideways.

"Oh, all right. The charity was for guide dogs for the blind; and my mother trained pet behaviourists."

He could see Lily was trying very hard not to smile triumphantly. He had to admire her for trying, even if it was annoying as hell that these massive coincidences helped bolster her ridiculous arguments.

"You mentioned your fiancée, Diane," Lily said hesitantly. "What about her?"

"What's *she* got to do with it?" he demanded. "I thought we were talking about genetic dispositions here."

"Also that the Compeers and their descendants probably, consciously or unconsciously, flock together. What was Diane's occupation? Did she try to get you to communicate with animals? Maybe she was attracted to you because you were working with dogs such a lot." Lily paused. "Oops, sorry. I didn't mean that to sound as though she might have only been interested in you because of you working with dogs. Of course I mean she would have been interested in you as a person as well. Or, I mean, first off, interested in you as a person…" She coughed and studied her hands. "But anyway," she tried again. "I was wondering what Diane might have been. Occupation-wise."

"Nothing to do with dogs!" But, Matt wondered, had Diane only been interested in him because of his career? He had wondered it before but more along the lines of wondering if she was only interested in him because of the lifestyle and money his career afforded him. He'd never considered it might be because he had a lot to do with dogs. Surely that wasn't possible, was it? He shook his head. He couldn't believe he was starting to consider this silliness!

"She'd have made a brilliant veterinary nurse," he muttered, much against his will, stroking Amber almost feverishly. "Why didn't I see that? Well, I did see that, but why didn't I do something about it? She'd have been happier then. Maybe she'd have stayed then."

"She might have done," Lily said. "But she might not have done. But if she did, she should have stayed for you, not for what you could have done for her. Also, if she wanted to be a veterinary nurse she could have done it herself. She didn't have to have you sort it all out, surely." Lily's colour was heightened again and she looked down as though she realised she'd not been as tactful as she might be.

"So what about you? You're a greeting card designer, and producer, and packer, and deliverer – as far as I can make out. What's that got to do with dogs? I mean, I suppose all this carry-on means that you're also a Compeer or the descendant of one."

"You're right, that's what I am – I produce my own greeting cards. But – and I didn't know why before all this carry-on as you call it – all the cards depict dogs."

"But surely you must know why. Why would someone who's grown up without ever having a dog or anything to do with the canine world, suddenly start painting pictures of dogs when she needs to earn a living?"

"I identified a niche in the market? I think that's what I thought at the time. In fact, I know it is. I did all kinds of fancy graphs and management accounting and all that to make sure it was a good idea."

"And your parents – did they approve?"

"No, of course not! But I thought they disapproved because being an artist isn't a 'proper job'. I don't remember it having anything to do with the subject matter. And anyway..." She picked at her nails in a way that made him want to hold her fingers to stop her doing it. She had pretty hands. "Anyway, they're not my parents as it turns out, are they? Or she isn't. Seb said so. Both of them were always distant. I can't say that one seemed more like my parent than the other. And now I want to know where my birth mother is and why she's not around any more."

Matt could think of nothing helpful to say about that. What could he possibly say about a dog telling Lily that her mother wasn't her mother? He wanted to change the subject before he got too far down the line towards appearing to believe this rigmarole!

Trying to look sympathetic, he opened the door into the surgery and stepped into it as if into a sanctuary away from all the madness. Amber slipped through with him. He closed the door behind him and leaned against it.

"Matt! Thank heaven you're here," Sandra, his veterinary nurse said, startling him. He'd thought he was alone. "Where have you been? What's been going on? All the police and everyone have gone, but I think there's still someone out there watching the house, so I'm not sure you'll be safe here. What are you going to do?"

"If you could put up a sign saying that due to er, illness, or circumstances beyond our control, the surgery will be shut for the time being, that would be great."

"I've already done that. I couldn't think what else to do, especially as I didn't know how to get hold of you."

"Thank you, Sandra. Good thinking. Sorry I've been out of touch. I've lost my phone. Along with everything else in my life, I might add." Amber leaned into him and flicked her tongue out over his hand as if to console him and make his sudden wave of self-pity ineffective. It made him feel better. He fondled her head and leaning over her he murmured into her fur: "Thank you, Amber."

"Thank heaven for that! I've waited and waited for the light to dawn," Sandra said grasping his arm in an altogether far too familiar way.

"What do you mean?" he said. He frowned and moved slightly away from her. It was enough. Sandra dropped her hands as though burnt and blushed furiously.

"The light *hasn't* dawned, has it?" she muttered.

There were tears in her eyes, but Matt was disappointed. He'd always thought her so sensible, so perfectly suited to being a veterinary nurse – not one of these soppy individuals for whom indulging in their own sentimentality came before doing what was best for the animal. And now here she was joining the, we-talk-to-the-animals brigade!

"Look, Sandra. I'm sorry if I've given the wrong impression to some people. I need to sort things out and then we can put all this nonsense behind us and get back to work."

"Give the wrong impression? Is that what you call springing someone from lockup?" Sandra said, rapidly recovering her usual robustness.

"That was an accident," he said. "At least, it wasn't premeditated, and as it wasn't deliberate then it must have been an accident."

Sandra snorted. "An accident! Is it also an accident that your nearly-in-laws have told the police they think you've got something to do with Diane's disappearance? Or that you've been selling drugs to people you shouldn't be selling drugs to?"

"What? How ridiculous!"

"Of course it's ridiculous. But all they need is some trumped-up charge either of wrong-doing or of mental incapacity and they can get you off the streets. They can get you away from all the people who need you to find them."

"Oh. We're back at this talking to the animals thing are we?" he said, sighing heavily. The tiny speck of doubt he'd felt talking to Lily earlier was now a large immoveable boulder in his stomach. Doubt of his own senses. Doubt of his own reasoning. There were so many people trying to get him to believe this nonsense, including Sandra – someone he'd known for ages and always thought the epitome of sense and reason.

"Seriously, Matt. Why do you think you have such a very large proportion of dogs in your practice? It's a much larger proportion than any other vet's practice in Bristol. And make sure to count in all the 'other' patients, too, the homeless dogs you treat without charge at your back door. You think no one knows about that, but they do."

Matt hadn't realised Sandra had known – she wasn't even around when it happened as he only did it outside surgery hours after she'd gone home.

"We all know about it," she said. "When I say 'we all' I mean us Compeers, those of us who have come to our senses and realised what we are – we form quite the community although there aren't that many of us, sadly, and we have to be very careful because of the ones who don't want us to survive or to realise what we are. We've been waiting for such a long time for someone to show us how to go home to the Realm and that someone is you by the looks of it, or maybe your friend, the one you got out of The Haven."

Matt didn't know what to say. It was a shock to realise that she must be in the same conspiracy with Lily. He'd thought Sandra was **his** friend as well as his employee. He hadn't realised she knew Lily at all. But she looked so bereft he couldn't help himself, he took her hands in a way that he never would have before. It was probably Lily's influence. She was a bit of a touchy-feely person. He hadn't liked it to start with, but maybe he was getting used to it.

"Sandra, if there was any way in which I could help you, I would. But I can't hand out false hope about talking dogs. I'm sorry. I'm a scientist. You can't seriously expect it of me. But I hope you know that if there is anything I can do to help, I will."

"I know," she said. She pulled one of her hands free and patted his arm with it. "I know you would help if you could. And I know you **will** help when you do finally see the light. I just have this horrible feeling we're running out of time. One of our people, that is, a Compeer, was killed last night. They're saying it's an accident but I don't think it was. I think we're all in danger. Something's coming to a head so I really hope you get it sooner rather than later."

He tried hard to keep the exasperation out of his voice. "Thank you for having such confidence in me, Sandra. It means a lot." He stuffed his hands hard in his pockets conscious of Amber watching him. She looked sad. Aarghh! How can a dog look sad? He was beginning to lose his way if he thought a dog looked sad or thoughtful or sarcastic or any one of those other things he was supposed to think if he was apparently, 'in his right mind'. He *was* in his right mind! Which meant the dog couldn't be looking sad!

He stormed out of the surgery, marched past Lily and Seb in the kitchen and kicked open the back door meaning to hide in the garden which was overgrown enough to conceal a football team, but he got no further than looking out beyond the conservatory because there was an orderly queue of people with their dogs quietly waiting for him. Of course, it was a Sunday! This was one of the main times when he tended to his 'other' patients.

Surveying the hope on their faces – the humans, not the dogs – he knew he had to buckle down, put all personal issues aside, and do what he could. He stepped back inside. "Clear the decks," he shouted. Lily and Seb jumped to their feet, looking eager. "I mean," he said. "Get out. We have business to attend to in here." Seb and Lily glanced at each other and shambled out of the room in the direction of the hall and the front of the house. Matt waved his first patient in and addressed the rest: "If you'd like to wait in the conservatory, at least you'll have a bit of protection from the weather." There was a general scramble for the rest of them to get indoors and the overflow edged into the kitchen and flattened themselves against the walls.

Sandra came into the kitchen. "I'll help."

"There's no need."

"I want to help. And it will make things quicker. Considering you shouldn't be here it would be a good idea if you finished up and left as soon as you can. Don't argue. Let's just get on with it."

Matt knew that mutinous jut to Sandra's jaw and she was right. There was a limit to the time he could be here without getting caught. It had been rash to come here in the first place.

Sunday evenings had become an odd time for him, one which he welcomed, but at the same time made him feel uneasy. Without analysing it too closely, he felt in communication with the world in a way he wasn't in his usual, tidily organised, routine surgery hours – as if on

Sundays he dealt with ***real*** people and ***real*** dogs instead of people who didn't quite connect with the Earth, and indeed barely skimmed its surface. A lot of people in his usual, 'normal' surgeries didn't even want their dogs to smell like normal, healthy dogs – they'd rather they smelled of lavender or patchouli. He snorted and startled Sandra. She looked up from laying out surgical instruments he might need, and raised an eyebrow. He shook his head and finished washing his hands.

Tonight there was the usual run of flea and worm treatments and one tick – Matt was amazed there weren't more of them! But there was also an unusual number of actual wounds.

"What's going on, Bert?" he asked one of his regulars, as he sewed up a great flap of skin hanging off his Queenie's shoulder. "This looks like she was in a fight, the last thing I'd expect of your Queenie."

"I dunno, Boss. I've never seen anything like it. It was a huge, grey thing. Thought it was a human to start with but it was dark and my sight's failing. Turned out to be some loose cur and it just went for my Queenie. Whenever other dogs have gone for her in the past she's just submitted to them and got away scot-free. Something about this one, though, and she was up there, teeth bared, fur all fluffed up, she scared even me." Bert's voice wavered and he stopped and patted his dog's leg. "I think she was protecting me. She must have thought it meant me harm. I wish she hadn't. I wouldn't have wanted her to be injured. As far as I'm concerned it's my job to protect her, not the other way around." He sniffed and wiped his eyes.

Matt concentrated even harder on making his stitches even while Bert recovered himself. "You might find a few like us here tonight, Boss," Bert continued. "That thing's been around the neighbourhood and tangled with a few. It even mauled Old Harry and he had to go to A&E to get fixed up. There were others, too, but they wouldn't go near the hospital unless they were carried in unconscious, so they must still be out there in Dog knows what state. But Old

Harry wasn't worried – then... Bet he is now. They locked him up!"

"Locked him up?" Matt knotted the last suture, fully closing Queenie's wound, and asked: "In A&E? Why would they lock him up?"

"They did, Boss. They nobbled him and carted him off. He's out at The Haven now. Yes, he went into hospital to get some wounds dealt with and ended up in The Haven. Why would that happen? I know Harry – there's nothing wrong with his mental capacity. And what's happened to Judy, his dog?"

Bert bent to hug Queenie. Standing straight again he opened his mouth, but before any words came out Matt got a very bad feeling. If he could have stopped the old man saying what he just knew he was going to say, he would have. But nothing on Earth was going to prevent it.

"They reckoned he was talking to his dog," Bert said. "They reckoned he and Judy were having a right old argument at the scene when the ambulance turned up. Harry was trying to warn them of these things, these Crules and their dogs, that is, their Curs –they are everywhere just now and dangerous. So they locked him up, what with him being homeless and all, with no one to stand up for him. They reckon he injured himself. They reckon he's a danger to himself."

And there it was. Someone else saying about people talking to their dogs, and Crules, and stuff he'd been bombarded with by Lily and Sandra. But this was from Bert, a homeless man who had absolutely no reason to come out with it. Unless he was also in league with Lily... But that was pushing it way too far and now he was getting paranoid. Maybe, he, Matt Lannings, was the one who should be locked up! Except that it was the world that was losing its reason around him and he was the only one left with his.

He tried very hard not to do it but something stronger than him made him turn to Bert with Dog knew what expression on his face because Bert appeared to shrink away a little before him. "Do you know Lily Wilkins?" Matt demanded. "Have you been planning this with her?"

The retreat from him was a definite physical movement this time and Matt was saddened that he'd caused it. "No, Boss. I don't know any Lily Wilkins. What would I be planning?"

Horrified that Bert was afraid of him, Matt gritted his teeth and forced himself to try for a jovial tone: "Sorry Bert – it's all this talk of people arguing with their dogs. Lily reckons she does that with hers. Actually, I've heard her do it – or rather, seen her do it – I've never heard him answer back, though. Haha." Matt fiddled with his scalpel and made himself put it down before he damaged someone with it. "I'm beginning to wonder if people aren't playing a practical joke on me."

He couldn't bear to look at Bert for fear of what he might see and he bent further over Queenie and pretended to check the stitches again.

"It's no laughing matter, Boss, when you get locked up for it," Bert snapped. "Old Harry might never come out of there now. I've known people get locked up and literally disappear. As for Judy – she's breaking her heart up there in the field outside The Haven waiting for him to come out. It's sad. That's what it is. Sad. Not funny at all." Bert fished in his capacious pockets for his hat and crammed it on his head. "When can I come for Queenie?" he demanded. "And how much do I owe you?"

"She'll be okay to leave here in a couple of hours. You don't owe me anything."

Bert ran his hands over Queenie's head and briefly dipped his face into the fur on her neck. He wouldn't look at Matt. "I'll be back in a while," he mumbled and slipped out of the back door.

Matt couldn't bring himself to look up. He knew exactly what expression there would be on Sandra's face. How come *he* was disappointing everyone? Someone had to be the voice of reason amongst all the hysteria. He almost didn't have the strength to carry on with his self-imposed veterinary duties but knew he had to. Before Sandra could get to it, he opened the back door into the conservatory and yelled: "Next!"

Bert had been right. There were several dogs with ugly gashes, far more than usual. Some of their humans were badly off, as well. They all shook their heads when he said they should go to A&E. All Matt could do was offer them dressings and turn a blind eye to whatever Sandra was doing in her little office at the back. He didn't want to know. He was pretty certain he'd lose his practitioner's licence if he did know. Sandra wouldn't let people out into the night with gaping wounds, though, so he let her get on with it. Anyway, he had his hands more than full with the dogs. It wasn't his job to tend to humans.

He wondered if Bert had said something when he left, clearly annoyed with Matt as he had been. Usually people were chatty, but not tonight, and he ministered to their dogs – their Compeers in the real sense – in complete silence. He missed their confidences, but as he was only there to help the dogs, he would cope. After another hour had dragged on like this, a palpable stirring like a wave of energy spread through the conservatory; even the air seemed fresher and full of anticipation. A knock on the door was followed by two heads peering around at him – Lily and Seb.

Matt glanced up: "You can't come in here," he said, and immediately looked back again at his patient, a lurcher of immense proportions called Yellow whose ear had been largely ripped from his head.

Lily ignored him. No surprise there then. She advanced into the room, Seb glued to her side. "Where's Sandra?" she demanded. The office door opened and Sandra stood in the doorway, a bloody swab in her hand, a look of apprehension on her face. "I'm here," she said. The lurcher's human, Mellow, loomed behind her, one hand cradled protectively in the other.

"Oh, thank heaven! I was afraid you were outside. Just stay in here. All of you! Think good thoughts!" And Lily and Seb, followed by Amber, swept out of the back door into the night. For an instant Matt thought something had surged in to take their place, something dank and heavy and foul. He shook himself, furious at his own fanciful idea. He was a scientist. Enough of such rubbish! Then he caught sight of Sandra's face again.

"Sandra, what is it?" he asked. He wanted to rush forward and catch her before she fell, but Yellow's ear was at a crucial stage. He looked at Mellow and snapped, "Get her a chair!"

"They're in my head," Sandra moaned, leaning over her knees; she grabbed fistfuls of her hair and pulled violently as if to get something out of her skull. Mellow knelt on the floor in front of her mumbling soothingly: "They can't get you. They can't get you."

"Who?" Matt wanted to know. "Who can't get her? Who? How can they be in her head? What the hell?" It was so frustrating trying to deal with people who refused to deal with what was in front of them – what was real, solid; what could be seen.

He concentrated on Yellow's ear and finished sewing it up in record time. As he clipped the final stitch the door flew open and smashed into the wall behind it. A cloud of bleak despair boiled into the room harassed by several dogs all with bared teeth and wild, desperate eyes. Transfixed, Matt stood immobile as darkness enveloped him and desolation took root in his mind. He'd always known there was no point to anything. He'd **always** known it! It was no wonder Diane had left him. Why would she stay when there was nothing worth staying for?

He brought his scalpel up and stabbed it in to his own throat. Again and again he stabbed. Or he tried to. Something stopped him. Something that hurt. But, nothing was going to stop him. Nothing! He looked down. Yellow had his teeth firmly in his elbow and was hanging on like grim death, his full weight on it, all his paws off the floor. Bugger! Was he up to date with his tetanus booster? And the wretchedness left his mind as if it had been switched off.

A howl of rage and frustration tore through the room and the deathly whirling abyss of nothingness had gone. The night was punctuated by gasps and sobs and the sound of approaching cries and barks from outside the room. The door was again thrown open, again punishing the wall behind it, and Lily stood there, hair sticking out from her head in spikes, blood smeared over her face, rips in her clothing. Seb clung to her legs as though he would never leave her side.

Amber galloped into the room, stopped when she saw Matt standing, scalpel in hand, blood dripping from his elbow; Yellow looking sheepish crouched on the floor as though he awaited a beating. The look in Amber's eyes told Matt that, yes, he now believed. He didn't know quite what he believed, but he believed something that he hadn't before. He could swear that warm approval flooded his mind wiping away all lingering traces of the despair that had taken root only seconds ago. Mellow found him a chair, too, and Sandra, now recovered, started to fuss over his elbow.

Matt could only look at Lily dumbly, too shocked by the influx of too many illogical things that he now knew he would have to take on board. He shook his head as though that would make everything in it settle down and give him some peace. It didn't work.

"What the hell was that?" he shouted in frustration. He knew he would never die by suicide. Not in a million years. And yet he also knew that if not for Yellow he would now have a scalpel jammed up to its handle in his throat, and at that particular point in time that had been exactly what he'd wanted. But yet he knew he would **never** do such a thing. He bent over and caressed Yellow until the lurcher stopped trembling and laid his muzzle on Matt's hand.

"A Crule," Lily answered him.

Matt sighed and straightened up. He knew he was going to be sorry he asked. He asked anyway: "And what exactly is a Crule?"

"It's a human being gone bad. They have no compassion, no feeling for others, no interests except their own."

"It didn't look very human."

"Once they're that bad they can be difficult to recognise. They present the image they want the world to see, whatever suits them at the time. They're everywhere and they can make life seem not worth living. That's often how they kill people – that is, they get them to kill themselves."

"This thing didn't look at all like a human being."

"They can appear to be human when they choose but they have to work quite hard at it. Usually they appear as this one did tonight as what they are – that is, an abyss of cruelty."

"An abyss of cruelty... oh, come on – you can't see an abyss of cruelty!" Matt was recovering himself a bit and he'd never had much time for all that poetry that didn't rhyme and literary fiction and pictures that weren't recognisable and stuff. An 'abyss of cruelty'! He snorted. Then he realised he was the target of many stares as though *he* was the one being ridiculous.

"So, tell me Matt," Lily said in a patient tone of voice that made him feel like he was six. "What exactly *did* you see? Or should I say, what exactly did *you* see?"

"Well, it was like a... a... nothingness, a void."

"Like an abyss."

"Not necessarily. An abyss is like something you might fall into."

"You didn't feel like you might fall into this nothingness, then, this void? You didn't feel like it was trying to make you *feel* like you might fall into it?"

"Well, yes. But an abyss is a real thing."

"So this nothingness, this void, wasn't *real*?" Lily stared pointedly at the scalpel he'd dropped into the kidney dish, and at his elbow, which Sandra had finished working on, and was now dressed in a neat bandage.

"Well, yes, but... Oh, all right. It was an abyss! A whirling, screechy abyss thing."

And suddenly, he was being looked upon with approval by all in the room. A cheer even went up from outside. He felt absurdly pleased, as though he'd just won his first scout badge – for admitting to the existence of a whirling, screechy abyss thing. "But the cruelty bit – how can you call it that? 'Cruelty' isn't even a thing, is it?"

And just as suddenly, the temperature in the room fell again and all the faces, furry, and non-furry looked at him as though he'd just taken his first scout's badge and defaced it with a felt-tip-drawn moustache. He tried a smile, a reconciliatory smile, but his face merely twitched with effort and the smile never came to fruition, just a showing of his teeth. His audience continued to watch him, singularly unimpressed.

"Well, Matt. And how did you feel when the whirling, screechy abyss thing had you in its power? Did you feel all warm and loved? Did you feel all triumphant and successful? Did you feel attractive and worthy? Did it make you feel good about yourself?"

"You know it didn't," he muttered.

"The reverse of all those things. Yes?"

"Yes! The reverse." He knew when he was beaten. He would just give in and let her get on with it. And he'd get her back later, somehow, not that he felt at all childishly miffed about it. Oh, no! "I felt the reverse of everything good and worthwhile," he declared.

Lily threw him a suspicious look, but she was on a roll... "And, Matt... Do tell us whether a whirling screechy abyss thing would make you feel like that because it was cruel, or because it was kind."

"Because it was cruel," he said expecting at least a pat on the head from his tormentor but when nothing came he tried again. "Because it wasn't a kind, whirling screechy abyss thing, but because it was a cruel, whirling screechy abyss thing." Lily still didn't look at all impressed with him. She was going to be a very difficult person to please, he could tell. Matt shifted his feet. He didn't like the atmosphere of growing expectancy. But he knew he could do this one last thing. "Because it was an abyss of cruelty," he whispered.

And once again he could bask in the warm approval of his fellow conspirators, his little gang of wanted criminals who talked to wild, hairy animals and flouted the law just whenever they possibly could. He was just where he'd always wanted to be in life – outcast and wanted by every authority known to humankind. The nose pushed into his hand by Amber, and the warm weight of her against his legs told Matt he was in exactly the right place, and he smiled, a great heaviness he hadn't known he carried falling from him. And he knew that for the first time in his life he could be himself now instead of what other people wanted him to be.

He could just be himself. Whatever that was.

"So, the Crules are after us," he said. "How do we protect ourselves against them?"

"It'll be easier now you know what you're up against," Sandra said. "You can be on guard against anything that makes you feel as though life's not worth living."

"And you have backup from any of us who happen to be around. It's probably best to make sure you go nowhere alone. This is what Compeers do, you know – they help to keep us balanced and hopeful. They keep us from loneliness and make us consider others. They keep us from the dark side." Everyone stared at Lily and she blushed. "It's Seb!" she said. "I'm only repeating what he's saying. That's all. Let's face it, I wouldn't sound as poncey as that, would I?" She yelped as Seb nipped her ankle.

"I want to make sure Judy is okay," Matt said. "And maybe break Old Harry out of The Haven. After all, it's presumably because of us that these attacks have taken place so I feel it's up to us to protect our own."

Unreality engulfed him. He was talking about 'our own' as though he had a family, a place in the world that he belonged. He hadn't had that for a long time. It was all very well, but if something could take over his mind to the extent that he would try to kill himself, who was to say that something couldn't take over his mind to the extent that he was made to feel all warm and fuzzy and Doctor Dolittleish? Where was *he* in all this? Where was the real Matt Lannings?

He's right here. For the first time in his life the real Matt Lannings is right here.

He knew that voice. It was oh, so familiar, although he'd never heard it before. Amber gazed at him and her certainty became his and he knew that he actually **was** himself for the first time in his life. He turned away and wiped his eyes on his sleeve, unnoticed by the others because Amber chose that moment to have a coughing fit.

"Thank you," he tried to say in his mind, groping his way into an unaccustomed communication.

You're welcome, she said. And he slid into his new life like a dolphin into a wave. Everything that had been missing was now present; everything that had felt wrong was righted. He was Matt Lannings and he could talk to the animals. He laughed aloud, and those around him turned to look in surprise. He hadn't previously been prone to laughing aloud in triumphant fashion.

"Right. Let's get Old Harry and Judy," he said, and started to fill a bag with supplies he might need. He wasn't sure Judy would come away if he couldn't get Old Harry out, and she might be injured. He threw in some food, too. Then he noticed Lily putting her jacket back on and he said, "No, it's just me that'll go. Too many people will be too noticeable out there."

"What if you get attacked? They're looking for you now. You'll probably be followed when you leave here. We're coming."

Matt had a strong, negative vibe about the possible outcome of arguing with Lily. So he didn't bother.

"What do you want me to do, Boss?" Sandra asked. She looked like she was about to salute. Although he preferred it to her usual argumentative self it was a bit too much of a change for his liking. As though he'd just been promoted to general overseer of the whole shebang. He really didn't want that promotion!

There were still a few people and dogs in the conservatory but he knew he'd already dealt with the worst injuries.

"Can you make sure everyone else is all right, please?" he said. "If you don't light up the front of the house you could keep them here, sort out any other problems they might have, feed them. Then at least you'll have protection, too. I don't know what's going on, or what we're going to be doing, but I am sure that, first, we need to do something about Old Harry and Judy."

Filled with an urgency he didn't understand, Matt finished packing his bag, snatched up his car keys and ran out into the street only to find that his car had been clamped. It was becoming apparent to him that Crules and their supporters had influence in every area.

"Here, Boss."

Sandra was at his elbow waving a set of keys. "Not up to your usual standard of motorised conveyance, but it has wheels and an engine." She pointed across the street at her old jalopy; it crouched there ready and willing to take off, looking like she had enthusiastic brothers who'd souped it up.

"Thank you," he said, taking the keys and smiling at her. She'd always been a great nurse; always knew what he needed before he needed it. And here she was, at it again. She returned the smile and ran back into the house. Matt and company piled in and with a great roar, wreathed in a cloud of exhaust fumes, they took off down the street.

No one stopped them at the entrance to The Haven's grounds. In fact, there weren't any gates to it as though anyone was welcome to roam the place at any time. Vast fields surrounded the main buildings, some bordered by dense woods. They slowly drove the winding road around the property until Seb spotted Judy. Matt would never have seen her, she blended in so well with the oatmeal colouring of the seed heads that enveloped her in the gathering gloom of evening. She was motionless, staring at the buildings. He stopped the car in the cover of some trees.

"She's willing Old Harry not to give up, apparently," Lily explained. "He's very low and she's afraid he'll fall foul of the Crules. But she herself is failing. Seb doesn't know how long she will last. She was injured quite badly. We need to fix her up. Or, rather, *you* need to fix her up. Or we'll lose them both."

"How do you know this?" Matt wanted to know.

"Seb told me," she said in a tone of voice that let him know he should have known.

The trouble with the fields was that if someone watched from the buildings they could see anyone approaching from miles off. Maybe that was the point…

Matt thought Judy was staring at the part of the building Lily had been in. The fence seemed higher. Was it higher? Or was it just that it looked higher from this side of it? Whether it was or not, Matt was sure the staff would be watching rather more carefully than prior to Lily's break out.

"See if Seb can get Judy to come here. They'll see us if we try to get to her."

But she wouldn't budge.

Lily looked meaningfully at Matt's suit. He'd put it on yesterday to visit Lily in The Haven and it had been the only thing he had to wear when he left Barker and Ruby's house. He'd covered it with a white coat for surgery, but had removed that when he left the house.

"Pity about the suit," she said, handing him his bag. He wasn't convinced of her sincerity.

Without a word he took the bag, got out of the car, and made a crouching dash to the edge of the field, thankful that evening had gathered momentum and gloomed the sky. He flung himself on his belly to crawl through the grasses. It was more difficult than he'd expected, crawling. Next time, if there ever was a next time, he'd make sure he was clad in more suitable crawling gear. Encouragement flooded him. He glanced to his side to see Amber's face near his. He gritted his teeth and kept going.

Judy was very reluctant to give up her pose, but eventually consented to lie down so Matt could see to her wounds. They were much more extensive than he'd imagined. He wanted to take her back to the surgery, but already knew she wasn't going to leave until Old Harry left too. So he did the best he could, but knew as he was doing it that she needed proper attention in a suitably kitted-out surgery if she were to survive.

There was nothing for it. They would have to get Old Harry out. And if Judy's injuries were that bad, how bad were Harry's? Surely they couldn't be very bad if he'd been locked up in The Haven rather than put on a general ward at the main hospital. On the other hand, he was beginning to realise that when Crules were involved, nothing humane entered the picture.

But how to get him out? They couldn't break down the fence without major ructions, not to mention some industrial machinery. It was a sturdy fence despite its lack of height. They couldn't sign in as a visitor and get him out that way. They'd done that already and presumably the staff and the Crules would be on the lookout for a repeat of that performance. To escape, Old Harry would either have to run through the security doors if they both happened to be open at the same time, which was unlikely, or run away when out on escorted leave, if he had any. Or if he did as he was told and said everything they wanted to hear, they might let him go. But that would take too much time.

We need a diversion.

Matt had adapted to Amber's voice in his mind so easily he wondered if it had been there his whole life just waiting for him to realise it.

"A diversion…" he muttered.

"You want a diversion?" Lily queried. Matt flinched. He hadn't heard her approach through the grass. "We can give you a diversion. How big a diversion? When do you want it? Who are we diverting?"

"We need to divert the staff long enough to get Old Harry out."

"What? Like you did when you got me out?"

"I don't think we can do the same thing again. Surely they'll be on the lookout for that at least for a while. And also, we can't go in as visitors."

"I can," Lily said. Her confidence was mind-blowing.

"Don't be ridiculous! You can't go in as a visitor. You've only just got out of there. And not with their permission, just in case you'd forgotten. It's a stupid idea!"

"No, it's not," she said. She had that argumentative thing going on again. He watched in fascination. There was something about the way her whole face lit up as she became more animated, but he knew he mustn't encourage her even by listening. He opened his mouth to be more authoritative and she swept on. "The thing is that they don't really **see** patients. They wouldn't recognise me if I went up to the door and said, here I am – I'm your escaped patient come to visit Old Harry."

"It's a stupid idea!"

"No, it's not. They wouldn't recognise me **because** I was a patient there – they wouldn't expect me to show up as a visitor so soon after escaping. Well, any time, really. It's the only thing to do. We could go and get Sandra and get her to do it, but she's looking after everything back at your place and anyway, we're here. It won't be a problem. Honestly it won't. Also, it's nearly the end of visiting time. If we're going to do it at all we must do it now. And we need to do it now because Judy won't leave without Old Harry and she really needs treatment back at the surgery. Your field dressing isn't going to do much for her is it?"

He knew she was right. About the field dressing. But he didn't want her to risk so much. He was afraid for her, afraid she'd be caught and locked up for good. As he crouched there gazing at her, unable to say what he was feeling and not knowing how to stop her, she went.

In the gathering night he could just make out the disturbance in the grass as she crawled back to the road. Once there she stood up and strolled along it as though out for an evening constitutional. Then she disappeared behind the buildings and Matt's breath burst from him in an agonised rush. "You can't go!" he whispered uselessly.

The wait was awful. He couldn't take his eyes from where he imagined Old Harry to be. He and Judy stared at the buildings, each of them looking for their human.

Matt imagined Lily approaching the door, ringing on the bell, waiting, being let in the first door, having to say who she was there to visit, signing the book, waiting for the second door to be unlocked, stepping through and then being grabbed by some huge, brawny nurses, hustled away out of sight, injected and never heard from again.

Waves of soothing vibes swept his mind as Amber nudged her nose under his arm. He glanced at her, and her lovely tawny eyes instantly made him feel more balanced. It was that stupid girl, Lily, who had the power to unhinge him.

But there was no way! No way on Earth, after his experience with Diane, that he was ever falling for anyone again! Especially not someone as irrational as Lily!

He was in control of his life and he had no plans for falling in love with someone so unsuitable and so far from his ideal woman. No.

Aarghh! Matt rubbed his eyes hard with his knuckles and pulled his hair a few times but still the possibility was there that this irrational girl had made him like her more than he should, or wanted to. He must be ensorcelled – it wasn't too great a leap from talking dogs to some kind of magic or witchery being applied to him. That'd be it. He'd been bewitched.

Lost in contemplation of being under Lily's enchantment, it took Amber's forceful nudge for him to register two difficult-to-see figures strolling along the road like they were out for a pleasant amble before dinner. Judy's quivering presence beside him made him realise it must be Lily and Old Harry. Judy's tail thrashed through the grasses, sweeping the stems back and forth in a mini storm, flattening them. Matt assumed Seb or Amber must be stopping her bounding towards Old Harry, and giving the game away should anyone be watching. It was time to get back to the car, though, so they could all get home as soon as possible.

Matt scrabbled as fast as he could through the grass. This wasn't doing his hands, his knees or his suit any good at all, but needs must. Canine company kept pace with him as though to encourage him along.

Back at the car he pulled himself into the driving seat, turned the ignition and waited impatiently for the escapees to get in. The minute the doors slammed he let out the clutch and the car jolted forward. He tried really hard not to go too fast and attract unwanted attention, but it was difficult. Luckily they were out on the main road by now. He sighed heavily and some of the pent-up tension left him. He wasn't cut out for the life of a criminal. He slowed down and relaxed a little. Stopping at traffic lights, he glanced in his rear view mirror.

"Glad to see you," he said. "No difficulties then?"

And Diane's face appeared where he expected Lily's, and she said, "No, it was really easy. They were letting Old Harry out for an escorted walk to the local shop for cigarettes. Lily told me you'd be waiting and here we are."

Matt heard the words she said but could make no sense of them. He couldn't stop staring at that oval, perfectly formed face, those so-familiar features that he'd not seen since she'd disappeared. "Lily," he muttered.

"No, it's Diane," she said brightly. "Surely you remember – your ex-fiancée. It's not that long ago – only a couple of months. I don't believe I've changed that much."

"I know who you are! I want to know where Lily is." He watched as the immaculately glossed, pearly-pink lips opened, but whatever she said was drowned out by a cacophony of blaring horns, and engines being revved mercilessly. He tore his gaze from Diane's and looked around him. He was stopped at the traffic lights which were now green. Throwing the car into gear he scorched away, roared down the nearest left turn, and threw everyone in the car forward as he came to a skidding stop at the side of the road.

Turning around he demanded, "Where's Lily?" Now that he was looking he could see Old Harry and Judy in the front, Diane and Amber in the back, and no sign of Seb. "Where's Seb?"

Diane pursed her lips. "Aren't you glad to see me? I'd have thought you'd at least want to know how I am or where I've been or why I went?" A short silence followed. "Oh, all right then – Lily's on the ward. She's fine. She's where she wants to be. Of course, I knew straight away who she was. She didn't know who I was, but I soon put her right on that score. See, I knew she was coming for Old Harry. Old Harry knew she was coming from Judy. We were just waiting for her to turn up and when she did we left for the local shop and she stayed behind. No one will notice for a while because of the diversion she will cause. Yes, I'm a descendant of the Compeers, too."

Matt winced, and started the engine, pulling away and heading for home. He had to get Judy sorted out properly.

Diane merely raised her voice. "Oh my, haven't you got the message yet? Even though you now communicate with a dog? You're a descendant of a Compeer, for Dog's sake! Get to grips, man. The world can't wait for you forever. I waited long enough. I waited too long. That's why I left. I couldn't stick it any longer. All that guarded stuff, all that logic that denied you your true self. I know it was the way you were brought up, but weren't we all? Some of us managed to break away from our upbringing."

Matt's lips were stiff as though they'd break if he said too much. "Why hasn't Lily come out? You do realise she's wanted, don't you. They'll keep her in there forever."

"Don't be so melodramatic. It is interesting to see it – I can't imagine you being so worked up about anything. I've got more emotion out of you in the last five minutes than I managed in the entire time we were together. You really have seen the light haven't you? I won't be able to call you Flat Matt any more will I?"

"Lily…" he could feel Amber's soothing touch in his mind but he rejected it. Fear had a greater grip.

"Old Harry and I were about to go out on escorted leave to the local shop to get cigarettes, or that was our excuse. Filthy habit, but he refuses to stop. Lily showed up, marched to the window, and demanded to be let in just as we were about to come out. We were all in the bit in-between the double security doors. As she was about to sign the book she looked up and saw someone inside that she thought she recognised. I only know this because Seb was telling Judy who was telling Old Harry who was telling me."

"Right," Matt said, trying to get a picture of it all in his mind.

"Anyway, Lily went very pale and staggered as though she was going to pass out. We backed away. Didn't want her falling on us." Diane looked smugly down at her very slim, very petite self. She looked up briefly, saw something she didn't like on Matt's face and hurried on. "Because of the commotion they actually looked at her and realised who it was and so they caught her, took her in, jabbed her with some sort of chemical cosh. Like they do."

She glanced up again. "But she'll have a nice rest and she'll be out soon. All she has to do is behave well, tell them what they want to hear and she'll be out in no time. Oh, except that of course after she escaped last time they might want to make sure she is completely well before they let her out, I suppose."

"And you let this happen. You let them capture her again even though you knew she was there to rescue Old Harry? Aren't we all on the same side?" he demanded.

"Some of us are," she said sulkily, "But that's a bit rich coming from you. I spent eighteen months trying to get you on side, but you just completely ignored me. A couple of days with Lily and somehow you've 'got it'. Anyway, you keep on about her, but she wasn't so bothered about you – she *wanted* to be in there. She thinks she saw her mother."

Matt's mouth must have been open for a while because it felt dry. "Why don't you ever say the important stuff straight away instead of dropping little crumbs for me to scurry around after, and then try to piece them together?"

"What fun would that be?" Diane smiled broadly but in the face of Matt's glare her amusement faltered and died.

"Her mother?" he queried.

"Yep. We're pretty sure it's her mother. Lily had an old photo in her pocket which her father had given her yesterday, apparently. The rest of it was a bit garbled. Has she only just found out her mother isn't her real mother?"

"Yes," Matt said, with Amber's prompting. Had she? Poor Lily. That could explain some of the odd attitude shown by her 'mother' the other day. It might also explain some of the erratic nature of Lily's current actions, too.

By this time they'd arrived at the back of Matt's house and parked. Matt hurried around to Old Harry's door and carefully lifted Judy out. Diane went ahead to open the door but Sandra had seen them coming and was ready to welcome them when they reached it. She exchanged a meaningful look with Diane, but then fussed about with her usual efficiency to get Judy settled on the table, and the instruments Matt needed ready to deal with her wounds properly.

Diane continued as Matt got to work on Judy. "Honestly, Matt, don't think too badly of me. I don't believe you could have got Lily away from there for all the diamonds in Africa after she saw this woman."

Matt couldn't rid himself of the pictures in his mind of how doped Lily had been when he'd got her out of The Haven last time. How could she possibly function in that state? How could she survive?

"What were you doing in there, anyway? How very convenient that you and Old Harry just happened to be going out when Lily was coming in."

"Old Harry's my uncle," Diane said, somewhat stiffly. "I also volunteer there part-time so that I can keep an eye out for our people in there."

"Our people?"

"Yes. Us what talk to dogs, Matt. Us. You and me, and folk like us. Get used to it!"

"There's no guarantee they'd end up there, is there?"

"It's highly likely they will. Crules run that place and use it to lock up all kinds of people they find inconvenient. There are a few clawk-heads in there…"

"Clawk-heads?"

"People addicted to the Realm drug, clawkle," Diane explained. "But apart from them, most people in there are people like us, Matt. Something is changing and we're all feeling it so people who've been guarded by their upbringing for their whole life are beginning to feel something and they can't cope with it. Also, the Crules don't want them to cope with it. They can't afford to have all Compeers and their descendants realising what they are. They would lose control of their various criminal enterprises, not to mention their ability to use the Realm for their own profit. Lily's not a huge big deal. They're only excited about her now because she escaped. Fancy letting her go back in anyway. I don't know why you're blaming me."

"Ha!" Matt snorted, trying to imagine stopping Lily doing something she'd decided she was going to do. "It wasn't up to me. I'm not her boss in any way, shape or form. I don't suppose anyone is. But we need her out here. She's no use to us in there."

And I need to know she's all right, he thought, conscious that his worry for her was out of all proportion to his liking for such an irrational creature.

To stop himself dwelling on his anxiety about Lily, Matt changed the subject. "Where did you go and why? You just disappeared. Your family blame me for it, you know. And, really – 'Flat Matt'?"

"Is this really the time and place to go into that, Matt?"

"No, I suppose it isn't, but it was such an inconsiderate thing to do."

"Oh, you weren't hurt by it. Your pride was. Don't give me the broken-hearted spiel, or that deserted, betrayed look. You only really noticed me when I'd gone and then it wasn't because you loved me." She stared at him as if daring him to deny it.

He couldn't, but only because he'd never thought of it like that. She was right. He hadn't been broken-hearted – he'd been affronted.

"I missed you," he said, and realised that was the truth at least.

"I suppose that's something," Diane said. "I'll take that, but let's not go over it all. We need to think about the here and now and what we're doing about Lily."

He nodded to acknowledge their unspoken truce on the subject of her disappearance. They'd both been inconsiderate.

"When you say a lot of people can feel something is changing, how many of those people are in there?" he nodded his head back in The Haven's direction.

"Quite a few, but I don't know exactly," Diane said glancing at Old Harry who sat still, his hand on Judy's head, as though willing her injuries to heal faster.

"But there are other people in there, as well? I mean, people who aren't necessarily our people." Matt said.

"Yes. Loads, but I don't know why they're there. All kinds of shenanigans going on, I shouldn't wonder."

"So, what are we doing about Lily?" Sandra said, as though she couldn't contain herself any longer. "And what about Seb? Where's he? I can't believe you drove off and left them behind, Matt!"

"I'm new to all this skulduggery," Matt protested. "I'll try to catch up but don't forget I've spent a lifetime trying to be law-abiding and doing the right thing, so I might be a bit slow to start with."

"A bit slow? How about positively sloth-like?" Sandra said. "The most important person in this entire movement and you leave her behind in The Haven. It's unbelievable. As for 'doing the right thing'. You are only just beginning to do that. For heaven's sake – keep up!"

Matt felt a cold nose prod his hand, and gratefully fondled Amber's head. At least she was still there for him. He was getting soundly undermined by everyone else in sight. Almost sulkily he set about clearing up after Judy's treatment. At least she was looking perkier now she had Old Harry back. He was sitting quietly by the treatment table, incessantly patting her leg, a cup of tea in his other hand.

"So what are we doing about Lily?" Matt asked as he bent to his task.

"At least we have some sort of communication with her through Seb, and then through him to Amber and you," Sandra said.

"I'm not getting any messages so far," Matt said. He'd finished cleaning up. He set out his instrument tray for future use, hoping it wouldn't be necessary outside of normal surgery hours, but afraid it might be.

"Are you getting anything at all?" Diane asked.

"No, I'm not. I don't know if it's because I'm not accustomed to this mode of communication yet, or if there's nothing to get. But then, if she's been drugged up to her eyeballs again there isn't going to be any communication of any kind is there."

"Seb would know though wouldn't he? If that were the case?" Diane said.

"He'd obviously know if he wasn't getting anything from Lily, but could he tell if he was getting nothing because of a shedload of drugs, or because she's having to be guarded in there. Could he tell the difference?" Sandra asked.

"Oh surely he could," Diane said. "Surely, they'd be two different types of non-communication?"

"See – you don't know either, do you?" Sandra said.

"Also, if there are Crules about, Seb's not going to broadcast is he? Or he'll give himself *and* Lily away."

"So, out of at least three scenarios we have no way of knowing which it might be, this silence," Matt said.

"Why don't you ask Amber?"

"She's fast asleep now and I don't like to wake her up. I don't think she'd be asleep if there was anything to worry about at the moment, or anything we should be doing. Maybe we should take this opportunity to get some rest as well. I for one am shattered." He yawned hugely, nearly falling over with weariness.

Sandra hurried over. "You go to bed," she said. "I think tomorrow might be quite testing. I'll finish clearing up in here, and I'll get our guests something to eat. Don't forget – don't switch any other lights on in case they're still watching the house. Tomorrow we must find a new base for operations."

"Okay," he mumbled. He didn't need lights anyway. His eyes were already shut. Finding his bedroom Matt fell on his bed and only with a huge effort of will managed to lever his shoes off. They fell with a thud to the floor. "Here," he said, patting the bed beside him. A furry heaviness, warm and fragrant and comforting landed next to him. He put his arms around her and fell asleep.

Chapter Nine

The shock of seeing that face held Lily immobile. She stared at the space that appeared where she was sure her mother had been. Her birth-mother, not Carol. Her biological mother.

She wanted to see again the photo her father had furtively slipped to her just the day before, but she couldn't because it would look a very odd thing to do at this moment. The face that had made her pause was definitely significant in some way even if she was mistaken about it being her birth-mother. Seb had felt something, too – Lily was aware of the tension emanating from him – so the woman must be important to them both in some way.

Lily had still been in the gap between the two security doors at that point. In the same space were a man and a woman. The woman was overloud in everything she said; the man had a gnarled face and eyes that surely had seen more horizons than existed in the Human Territories. A slight inclination of his head to the great outdoors and she smiled at him, knowing it was Old Harry, hoping to reassure him. She knew her sudden decision to stay in The Haven was right. Of course it was!

Heck, heck, heck. Of course.

Lily didn't know who the woman with Old Harry was, but all that mattered was that they were going in the right direction. "Just going to the shop. Be back soon." The woman's voice was sing-songy and irritating. Again, Lily smiled at Old Harry. She couldn't leave here now she'd seen the woman she thought was her birth-mother. There were also these vibes that Seb was picking up, which might be important to their cause.

Lily's hand had wavered over the signing-in book. The nurse in charge of the desk, the opening of the security door mechanism, and the signing-in book had a huge silver thing around her neck, no doubt the height of fashion. Lily thought it looked more like something a plumber might use to unblock a drain. Fancy being allowed to wear something like that to work – it could surely be used as a weapon. Lily signed the book using her real name and pushed it back to Nurse Silver Lump who pulled it to her and, about to unlock the inner door, smiled in Lily's general direction.

Lily realised there could be melodrama if they stumbled to the fact that she'd escaped from here only a couple of days earlier. She couldn't afford to have them getting all uptight about it, and drugging her into a state that would render her useless for days on end. She had to engineer it so that everything could be calm and she remained in control of her own senses.

She burst into tears, and Nurse Silver Lump finally looked at her properly, looked at the book, saw the name, and checked it against the list taped to the front of her computer screen. Her mouth rounded in an almost-scream, but rapidly changed to sympathy as Lily continued to sob.

Ratcheting the sympathy-gathering up a gear, Lily added to her already forceful performance a wavery, but determinedly brave little voice: "I'm *so* thankful to be back here again. I was here yesterday and some man came to visit – he said he was my brother, but I didn't even know him." She gasped in a faltering breath and continued: "He came to visit and then when I didn't know what was going on, he abducted me. He threw me over the fence and someone on the other side carried me off. I was terrified. I managed to escape him but have only just found my way back here. You *will* help me won't you?" She ended on a hoarse whisper, her hand blindly groping to find Nurse Silver Lump's so she could hang onto someone who wouldn't let her down so very badly.

Matt would be okay about this, surely. What was a little case of abduction added to the list of crimes he was already wanted for? He'd be fine about it. Wouldn't he? Yeah. Of course he would.

Heck, heck.

Nurse Silver Lump's hand came out and grasped Lily's, while she turned in her chair and nodded to her compatriots behind her, letting them know she didn't need them after all, to subdue this escapee.

"Don't you worry, my dear," she said. "We'll get you sorted. Just you hang on and we'll get you a bed and sort you out. Everything will be fine."

Lily gave her saviour a weak smile of gratitude. Her mother, or whoever that face belonged to, still hadn't reappeared, but there was no other way Lily could think of to find out her significance other than to get back into The Haven. "Oh, I am so relieved. Thank you so much."

"Where have you been for the last twenty-four hours?"

"It's all been so confusing. I don't know where I've been. I spent the whole time either asleep, or drugged unconscious – I'm not sure which – or trying to get away. And then when I did get away it took ages to get here again. I didn't dare take public transport and I had no money for a taxi. Anyway, thankfully I'm here now and safe."

"He drugged you?" Nurse Silver Lump was aghast.

How ironic.

"Did he... you know...?"

Why were people so obsessed with sex all the time? Lily barely contained the curl her lips wanted to make of themselves. "Did he what?" she asked blankly.

"Oh, er, never mind. Come on through." And Nurse Silver Lump unlocked the inner door.

Lily stepped through, conscious that this might be a mistake, but seeing no other way to deal with the possibility that her mother might be in here.

Seb's presence in her mind increased warmingly and made her feel braver. Nurse Silver Lump appeared next to her. "Come along, dear. Let's find you a bed and a toothbrush. What a terrible man. After you're settled I'll report this about him too. Funnily enough I took my little Fluffybutt to see him. He's a highly recommended vet, you know. He's my Shih Tzu – Fluffybutt, that is, not your abductor – he has problems with his, well, with his rear end – Fluffybutt, that is. Fluffybutt's butt. Anyway, he seemed quite a respectable man at that point. Quite fanciable in many ways. Not that I fancied him. Not at all. Saw right through him in fact. Knew he couldn't be trusted. Could tell there was something not quite right about him. No. Fluffybutt liked him, but dogs are so unreliable in that way aren't they. They like everyone. You can't trust them."

Seb, if his complete silence was anything to go by, was stunned by these revelations. Stunned.

"I suppose the only time you can really trust a dog is when he dislikes someone," Nurse Silver Lump continued. "Then you're probably best to watch out for that person. But be careful when it likes someone because they tend to like everyone. Yes, I think that's probably true."

She might have something there. One of our major faults is liking everyone.

Nurse Silver Lump carried on down the hall, her voice rising and falling with her footsteps. Lily followed, all the while keeping an eye out for her mother.

Seb yawned jaw-achingly. Lily could feel him settling down somewhere, doziness overtaking him. She was glad he could relax and be so comfy while she was back on the knife-edge of danger, locked up and in the hands of control freaks.

That's why I can relax. You're not going very far, are you?

Hmphh!

Nurse Silver Lump was very easy company. She could hold a conversation all by herself. Lily spent the time grunting when she thought it appropriate, and scanning the halls and rooms they passed for her birth-mother's face, but failed to find it.

"And here's the public phone, but you've probably got a mobile. Everyone's got a mobile these days. Even though they're probably frying their brains with them. No wonder there are so many people needing to come in here. I've no doubt it's all to do with mobile phones. So they come in here and they use their mobile phones even more because the public phone is hopeless because everyone rings in on that one so there's always someone on it. And it smells. Not the phone. The cubby hole the phone's in. It smells of cat pee. Who'd want to hang around – you can't even sit down in there – in a place that smells of cat pee. You can't have the phone charger yourself though so you'll have to ask us to charge your phone for you."

"Cat pee? How does that happen? No, never mind. I don't care."

Zzzzzzzzzzzz.

Seb's snores reverberated through her mind. It was so nice to think he was relaxed enough for a nap while she was in peril of cat-pee-smelling cubby holes!

Lily nodded and smiled absently in Nurse Silver Lump's direction, her gaze flitting everywhere.

"And here's your room. You have to share, of course, but it's nice to have company isn't it? Yes, of course it is. You'll get along like a house on fire, the two of you. You'll probably be up all night talking and giggling like girls do. Maybe even have a midnight feast like in all those books you read when you were young. Pinch a few extra things at supper time for your midnight feast. Ay?" Silver Lump nudged her over-enthusiastically in the ribs.

Lily gasped out an affirmative little choking sound, which seemed to fit the bill, because Silver Lump was off again: "Of course, you can't really pinch things at supper. We wouldn't look too kindly on that. There wouldn't be enough to go round so it wouldn't be a nice thing to do and we'd have to report you. But you won't do that, will you? Actually, we don't approve of midnight feasts either. Anyway – where's your bag?"

Nurse Silver Lump looked all around her as if Lily's bag was going to creep out of a cupboard and present itself, or maybe it was hiding behind the curtains.

Lily managed to shake her head.

"You don't have a bag? Well, we'll have to see what we can find for you won't we? Toothbrush and so on. Why haven't you got a bag? Everyone has a bag."

"Uh, well, I was too busy getting away from my abductor and lying low and trying to get back here to think of such practicalities, but on the whole I would agree. Everyone should have a bag."

Nurse Silver Lump looked at her suspiciously for rather too long and Lily realised that, regardless of the endless waffle, this wasn't a good person to cross. She tried her best at a pathetic little I'm-lost-and-without-a bag look which seemed to work because Silver Lump stopped with the stabbing stare, grabbed her arm and marched her off down the corridor to the lost property cupboard. She rifled through it, flinging out things every now and then, deciding they would do.

"And these," she grabbed some dungarees. "These belonged to a sad little woman, Cynthia, who was always trying to escape. She was actually homeless and chatted incessantly to an invisible dog. They brought her in here to give her a break from the streets. She couldn't stand the hostels. Places full of danger. And this," she shook out a frilly little number more appropriate for a cocktail party than a locked ward. "This belonged to that Anita. She was no better than she should be, that one." A dark look was sent Lily's way, presumably to see if *she* was no better than she should be, either. Lily tried hard for a naïve, hurt look and Silver Lump bent to her task again.

All these things were in a heap on the floor of the cupboard mixed in with shoes and carrier bags full of half eaten snacks and opened tobacco pouches, as though the door had been opened, stuff had been flung in without looking, and the door had been shut again. Why didn't the owners take their stuff with them when they left?

Possibly because they left unexpectedly over the fence and didn't think to rush back inside first to grab a bag...

Lily decided she wasn't ever going to get undressed again and would live the rest of her life in the clothes she already had on.

Finishing her task to her own satisfaction, even if to no one else's, Nurse Silver Lump straightened up with a groan, a theatrical hand on the small of her back. "You don't know it yet but when you get to my age you'll be sorry you didn't look after yourself when you were your age. If only I'd known the damage I was doing to myself I would have behaved differently, let me tell you."

Lily was tempted to let her tell her indeed, but was afraid if she asked a leading question the Niagara Falls of Silver Lump's oration would never stop, and her voice would be the last thing she heard as she fell into a coma. Even so, she was very tempted. What in all the world, the human world, that is, could Silver Lump possibly have been doing to herself? Lily would, however, let that particular mystery lie.

A short, tinny burst of 'Auld Lang Syne' made Silver Lump whip her phone out of her pocket. A glance at the message on its face and she said, "I've spent quite long enough with you. You've got everything you need now. It's teatime. You'd better get to the dining room if you want anything to eat. And just make sure you behave this time. And I'll be keeping a special eye out for any visitors you might have, too!" And off she marched to keep whatever assignation had been arranged via the marvellous medium of text.

Lily took the stuff she'd been given and dumped it on her bed. And then picked it up and put it on the floor. Some of it actually gave off quite serious odours...

Finding her way around the corridors she came to the dining room. Hovering in the doorway it was apparent that everyone had already got their meals, and found their cliques.

"Hurry up if you want anything, Luv," called a man from behind the counter. Lily smiled at him and asked for a baked potato. It was presented to her with some dubious looking chilli, and a few pieces of weary lettuce.

Looking around to see where to sit, she noticed a group of people crowd in more tightly together in a very we-don't-want-you-to-join-us way; a young couple beamed invitingly at her – they were wound together so tightly it was difficult to tell where one started and the other ended; one woman sat alone. Lily headed for her table, but was about a metre away from it when she clearly heard her say: "No, no. Don't want company. Want to be alone. Go away."

"Oh, okay," Lily said, backing off. Fair enough. If she didn't want company why should she have to have it? Turning around, she spotted the woman she'd been looking for, and headed for her instead. As she approached, her possible-mother got up and walked away.

"Over here," a voice called, rising above the chatter in the room. Lily turned to find its owner and there was her caller from a couple of days ago, a Crule posing as an old man reminiscent of her granddad, who'd come to her door looking for his dog.

Her guard came down so fast she realised she'd not had to think about it. It was good to know she could do it so naturally now, but it did leave her cold and alone without her contact with Seb. As for him, she got the fleeting impression of someone who'd been on the verge of slumber suddenly yelping with shock before she cut him off.

She smiled at the Crule and walked towards his table. It was full but as she approached one of the company got up, picked up his tray and moved to the next table as though making space for her.

"Hello there," she said, sprinkling her voice with pleased surprise. "How lovely to see you here," as though they'd met on a carefree summer's afternoon picnic, and he hadn't tried to manipulate her to his own ends. She placed her tray on the table and sat down, fussing with cutlery and the paper serviette. "Did you ever find your dog? How awful that must have been, to have lost him. I do hope you did find him."

"I didn't find him."

"Oh, how absolutely dreadful! I hope your wife is all right."

"No, she's not. She's devastated. As one might expect. He was like her child."

His monotonous tone didn't suggest too great a devastation however. Not like a locust-stripped soul of despair or a tragically bereft grieving woman – he made it sound more like someone had left their rug airing in the sun and went back to find a passing bird had blessed it. Lily expected a Crule to do a better job of deceit than this. She speared her soggy-looking baked potato and mushed it up a bit.

"I'm so sorry to hear it. So very sorry." She said, trying for a sympathetic look. What she really wanted to know was what he was doing in here, but she couldn't work out how to ask.

"That's why we're in here, of course."

"We?"

"Of course. The wife and I," he said, as though trying out the phrase for the first time. He said it again: "The wife and I do everything together. I wasn't going to let her go through this suffering by herself so I came in with her."

Lily was pretty certain it didn't work like that but she wasn't going to argue, and anyway, where Crules and their ilk were concerned the 'rules' of life didn't seem to apply. If they wanted to treat what she'd always thought was a local community hospital like it was a prison for some and a hotel for others she had no doubt they could do so.

"So you'll be able to tell her yourself how sorry you are," he said meaningfully. As if Lily had pinched their dog. Which in a way she supposed she had.

Looking around Lily could see no likely candidates for the position of Crule's wife so she could say how sorry she was. The rest of the people at their table remained silent and hunched forward as if to catch every golden word she and Crule should drop, but none of them fit the description of 'the wife' that she could see, unless it was the very young girl on the other side of the table with nails so long Lily couldn't imagine how she did anything without cutting herself.

"No, that's not her," Crule said, frightening Lily into wondering if her guard was properly up, or if she'd accidentally let it slip. "My wife is resting in her room. She's had a bad day today. Too many surprises. After supper I'll get her to come out and you can say hello."

"Don't disturb her on my behalf," Lily murmured wondering if the stuff she'd forked into her mouth had ever lived in the ground, or if it had been born in a test tube.

"She will come out to see you," he said, and Lily knew his wife would indeed come out to see her whether she wanted to or not. This immediately made her sympathise with 'the wife'.

"I'm sorry, but I don't remember your name from our last acquaintance. What do I call you? I'm Lily."

"I know who you are!" he snapped. "You can call me Credence."

She couldn't be bothered answering him. She was so very tired, she was missing Seb's support, and Credence's tone was so unfriendly the effort to overcome it was too great.

He must have seen it on her face because he tried again: "The food's not good is it? How can they expect people to get better if they can't even give them decent food? Don't worry. Don't force it down. After supper is done I'll get in a takeaway."

Like a takeaway was going to be full of natural goodness! Credence really did treat the place like a hotel. Lily made herself smile at him. He'd tried, and so should she. She gave herself a mental jab with a sharp elbow – she was in danger of thinking of him as a person. He was a Crule and she mustn't forget it.

When everything had been cleared away and numbers in the dining room dwindled as people drifted off to play cards or watch TV, or go to lie on their beds, Credence texted 'the wife'.

Somehow it came as no surprise to see her mother walking towards them. It was as if someone was handling a bunch of threads and they were all puppets in an unknown play. It had to be her mother.

She was way too young for this man, though, this Crule. She must be half his age! She sat down next to Credence with a little thump into the chair as though her legs could no longer hold her up. There was no life in her face at all.

Is this what happened if you were the descendant of a Compeer brought up with no communication in your life, no feeling, no empathy? You became completely guarded, uncaring and blank? This was her mother. She looked like a poor dab to Lily.

"Lily, this is the wife, Delilah. Sweetie, this is Lily. She's newly arrived here. We must make her feel welcome."

"Hello, Delilah," Lily said, receiving no response in return. She tried to muster some feeling in her heart for this woman, but it was difficult in her own guarded state. She didn't think it was just that – Delilah had never been there for her; Lily didn't know her. Why should she feel anything for her? The only emotion she could muster up was a faint idea of pity.

She smiled encouragingly in her mother's direction, but Delilah merely looked back with no flicker of recognition or interest.

Why the hell had she put herself back here under lock and key for the sake of this person, this non-entity? Lily vaguely wondered if she'd feel differently if she weren't so guarded, which she was finding very tiring, but at the moment she just felt stupid for putting herself in this position. The woman sitting opposite her now wasn't worth it!

With any luck she'd at least get a decent night's sleep. She was weary beyond measure. Tomorrow she'd work out how to escape – she was too exhausted to think about it now. She couldn't believe how tiring life was without Seb in her mind, how heavy her limbs felt and how difficult it was even to breathe without his uplifting presence.

"Well, it was lovely to meet you," she said in Delilah's direction. "And to meet you again, Credence. I'm very tired. I must go to bed before I fall over. I'll see you in the morning."

Again, there was no response from Delilah. Credence at least painted a polite smile on his face.

Lily shambled off, more exhausted than she could ever remember being in her life; she was beginning to doubt this whole business – it was all so unlikely and made no sense whatsoever. She'd just met her birth-mother and felt absolutely nothing about anything. So much for maternal feelings or daughter-feelings or the mother-daughter bond or any of that stuff. There'd been nothing at all on either side. Fancy meeting your own mother and feeling the same as if you'd exchanged a few words with your bed-post. That is – nothing.

Where was the point in it all? Lily could barely hold her head up by now, and desperately wanted nothing but to sleep. At the same time she was niggled with the idea that she wouldn't be able to sleep. It wasn't something that bothered her usually, sleeplessness, but there was definitely something gnawing away at her mind, something she knew for certain would keep her awake tonight when she so badly needed sleep.

Spotting Nurse Silver Lump, Lily pursued her down the corridor. When she finally caught up with her, she asked for sleeping tablets.

"Are you sure, Lily? You look done in already, if you don't mind me saying. You'll probably sleep like a log."

"No, I won't. I can feel something in my mind that's going to bother me all night long and keep me awake. I need my sleep so I want to make sure I get some."

"But…" Nurse Silver Lump said, then glanced past Lily's shoulder and her protests vanished in an instant. "Come with me and I'll get you some sleeping pills. You did the right thing asking. Don't hesitate to do it again. Whenever you want. Sleep is vital for health, you know."

They turned to go back down the corridor and Lily saw Credence standing there staring at them, a peculiarly smug expression on his face. Delilah stood behind him like some creature who had to hold onto his robes to survive; let go and she'd be finished.

A flutter of alarm made Lily hesitate but the weariness was like a living thing now and the niggle was as bad, getting really screechy and annoying in her head. She hurried after Nurse Silver Lump and gratefully threw the proffered sleeping tablets down her throat, washing them on their way with water and feeling almost immediately at peace. She'd sleep now. What a relief!

She shuffled back to her room and fell on her bed. Sleep overtook her like an avalanche. At the edges of her mind she heard howling, awash with despair and loneliness. It made her feel bad. Very bad. As though she were hanging onto the edge of a cliff, razor sharp rocks below waiting to rip her body to shreds when she fell. "Wolves?" she muttered. "There are wolves in Bristol now?" A renewed onslaught of nipping at her brain made her roll over trying to get more comfortable. "Nah. That can't be right. There aren't any wolves here." And she fell into sleep like she'd plummeted from the cliff, a last, desolate wail following her down.

Chapter Ten

The morning brought Matt new waves of indecision. There was an air of rudderlessness about them without Lily and Seb around being nuisances. He sat up and swung his legs over the side of the bed. Amber had already gone and her spot on the bed was cold so he must be late already. Immediately a reassuring presence in his mind made him relax. Even so, he leapt up, took a quick shower, found clean clothes, and feeling reasonably presentable for the first time in days, he joined the others in the kitchen.

Lily and Seb's absence was even more obvious when all of them were together, and worry hit him with renewed force.

Sandra leaned on his shoulder until he sat down. She thumped a plate stacked with bacon, eggs, tomatoes, mushrooms and fried bread in front of him. "Eat that," she commanded. "We have no idea when we'll get another home-cooked meal. We must leave here very soon. I heard on local radio early this morning that you didn't help Lily escape last week."

"I didn't?" he queried, taking in the full splendour of his breakfast feast and eagerly getting started on it.

"Nope. You actually abducted her, so we need to get away and find somewhere safe."

He'd been in the process of chewing a particularly tasty field mushroom. He choked, and coughed, and coughed, desperately moving away from Diane's not-too-gentle thumps on his back. Why do people do that? The last thing he wanted when he was coughing like crazy was someone hitting him!

"I abducted her?" he asked when he'd recovered, eyes streaming. He jabbed viciously at another unassuming mushroom. It made a dash for the edge of the plate and freedom on the floor, but Matt was quicker and speared it through the heart. At least he had power over that. He obviously had none anywhere else in his life. "So, I'm a kidnapper now as well," he said bitterly and stuffed the mushroom in his mouth chewing it savagely, delighting in its helplessness between his teeth. That'd show it!

He was never going to get his life back now! All his work, all his striving and studying, all his ambition, come to nothing.

"Yep. You're a very dangerous man it would seem and not to be approached by innocent members of the public." Diane seemed to relish his discomfort. "There's even a helpline for people who've been traumatised by your presence," she said.

Matt stopped chewing. Life was getting way out of hand!

"Nope. Kidding. Not the last bit. No helpline," Diane said. "But it is urgent that we get away forthwith! We've been watching those who've been watching us all night and we're okay at the moment, so finish up your breakfast, gather your things and let's get going. We'll go out the back. The others are waiting and ready to go." She said this so brightly Matt might have thought they were planning a trip to the seaside with bucket and spade, with the charabanc waiting outside packed with baskets of cucumber sandwiches and fizzy pop.

They crept out through the back garden, each of them carrying as much as they could and still run if they had to. Handily, Matt had quite a collection of rucksacks from previous walking holidays, from back when life was 'normal'.

When it came to weapons, they had none. It would have been nice to have a gun or a big knife but even whilst thinking it, Matt couldn't see how they could be used against such an enemy – not the Crules anyway, although they'd be useful for their Curs. As soon as he thought it he knew he'd have great difficulty knifing a dog, which was essentially what a Cur was. He cringed at the thought and hoped it wouldn't come to it.

At least they were in larger numbers now they had the 'other' surgery regulars, too.

"Where are we going?" he asked Sandra.

He was holding open the back gate for her so it didn't swing shut in her face. For some reason she was carrying someone else's rucksack and her hands weren't free.

"Need to know," she whispered. "You don't need to know." Matt nearly let the gate go, but prided himself on a restrained response. He hadn't lost all sense of civilization and decency even if he was a highly wanted outlaw with a price on his head and no longer had a career or even a home to call his own. No. He wasn't going to let the gate smack into her face despite immense provocation.

"I do need to know," he whispered back desperately keeping his voice down and not shouting at the top of his lungs like he wanted. "Or I won't know where I'm going, will I?"

"Just follow Diane," she said. "Why do you always have to be awkward?"

He let the gate slam shut behind him. Sandra was clear of it, but there was still some satisfaction to be had from such a rebellious act.

"Oy!" Sandra said. "Keep quiet! We don't want all the Crules in creation to find us, do we? Or the police? Or Lily's family. Or…"

"Okay, okay," he said, head down and resolving to follow Diane as he'd been ordered and do nothing else at all. Absolutely nothing. They'd have to ask him very, very nicely before he did anything for them now. A nose in the back of his leg made him snort with suppressed laughter. He'd been dangerously close to sulking. He used to sulk when he was little. But that was a long time ago. Gratefully, he put his hand back and found Amber's silky head. It was so solid and yet so soft and so comforting. He plodded on.

Matt had no idea where they were. Diane led them down some tiny little paths between houses, along the edge of some allotments, at one point they followed the river. It was weirdly quiet down there in the dip with the river flowing beside them, knowing that the great city of Bristol was just up the hill with all its traffic congestion and drama and violence. It was a bit of time-out. For a small moment his constant worry about Lily faded, his mind relaxed a little and tranquillity streamed in. He held his face up to the sun. It was weak but it was still the sun, and with no rain or biting wind, it was pleasant to feel it.

Ear-stabbing shrieks shattered his new-found serenity and without thinking he plunged forward, pushing people out of the way. A blur of red and cream whispered past him. Amber! He would never let anyone or anything hurt her again. Never! An unfamiliar determination flooded him and he knew his anger alone could defeat anyone who tried to harm his Hound or his people.

He roared in fury and smashed heavily into a dreariness physical in its solidity, soul-draining in its power, but Matt now knew better than to let it get a hold on his mind. He bellowed again and lashed out with his fists not knowing if he was hitting anything or not, but feeling the entity immediately receding before his anger. He registered somebody on the ground, blood streaming; someone else struggling in the river, splashing and screaming; and he turned to attack the creature again who now stood on the riverbank snarling and scything its giant claws into the water.

Amber struggled with three Curs; they had enormous jaws and she was taking a heavy toll. Bert was trying to help her, but they moved so fast it was difficult for him to hit one of them without hitting Amber. Matt sent her a rapid stream of strengthening vibes; he literally felt them strengthen her, and they returned and strengthened him.

Trying to avoid the body on the ground he tripped and fell into the blighted being on the riverbank. It initially shrank back before ballooning out and enveloping him in fear so great he couldn't breathe, couldn't move, couldn't think. But, no – he knew this – he'd been here before and no matter how he felt, he knew he had to fight whether he thought it would do any good or not, whether he was able or not; as long as he fought with everything he had he would be a winner. The knowing of it broke him free and with a flesh-freezing scream of rage the creature fled, its followers doing the same, and the attack was over as suddenly as it started.

They were left on the river bank in the peace of the valley below the level of the city, left to recover themselves as best they could. Hastening to Amber, Matt knelt on the ground, his trouser knee soaking up her blood. His head on her chest he willed health and harmony her way. Her wounds were already closing but they had been vast. Matt was hazy about how it worked but surely a body couldn't take this kind of battering and not be weakened somehow. Thank heaven Lily was safe in The Haven! At least she'd been spared this.

Diane told him the human body on the ground was Kevin the Hand, he of countless poker games that always left him roofless and shirtless. The wounds on him were superficial and she thought he might have had a heart attack. He was dead. Sandra was helping a woman called June from the river. She had suffered small injury, but a lot of soaking, and peppered the air with profanities.

The rest of them were surprisingly undamaged, but very shaken.

Sandra disagreed with Diane's pronouncement. "Kevin the Hand's heart will have been stopped by the Crule. It will have made him believe it wasn't worth going on so it stopped bothering. It's a typical despair-death."

"At least it looks like a natural death, whatever you want to call it," Diane said. "Which means we can leave him here and keep going. No one will come after us about it. At worst it looks like he was attacked by a couple of dogs and died of shock."

"We can't leave him here!" Matt exclaimed.

"What do you suggest we do with him, Matt?" Diane wanted to know. "We can't bring him back to life. We can't take him with us. If we stop to notify anyone we'll be caught by someone. You're wanted by every authority in the land. Tell me what you want us to do." She waited.

By this time they were clustered together fearfully looking over each other's shoulders – as if that would make any difference. Crules didn't exactly walk up to you and politely cough to let you know they were there – they just appeared as if out of the air and went straight into attack-mode. Matt kept feeling for Kevin the Hand's pulse even though he knew it wasn't there to be found. He was dead. Slain by a Crule.

Despite his own struggle with one, despite Amber's wounds, despite the anger and despair surrounding them, and the blood on the ground, Matt couldn't believe what had happened. He couldn't believe Kevin the Hand was dead. He stopped prodding his throat and held his hand instead.

Heavily dropping to the ground beside Kevin's body, Matt wondered how they could ever get through this. How could anyone, let alone a couple of clueless people like him and Lily, a Hound or two, and a motley lot of others deal with a force so determined and so deadly? How could they possibly hope to win? A sharp pain in his calf brought him to his feet, wildly searching around for the enemy, but all he saw was Amber, a loving but impatient look on her face. She'd bitten him?

Of course. Every pup needs nipping, Matt. This is what Crules do. They don't just attack when you can see them. They attack when you can't as well. And that Crule was just doing a very fine job on you. I must say, you're not as fast a learner as I expected you to be. She leaned into him, he put his arms around her and the sting in her words disappeared; he filled with love and confidence, and knew he could do it.

The tail end of a thought whispered though his mind: *I suppose you **are** a suitable mate for our Lily...*

"What?" Matt shouted, thunderstruck. But when he looked enquiringly at Amber she looked back at him with such dumb animal liquid eyes he knew he must have imagined it. He rubbed his face fiercely. Pull yourself together, Matt, he admonished himself.

"So what do we do with Kevin?" he asked.

"We can't take him with us, Matt," Diane said. "You know that."

"We can't leave him here. Did he have a dog?"

"I don't think he did."

"Does anyone here know anything about Kevin the Hand?" Matt enquired, raising his voice to drown out the rustling of the dried grasses in the breeze that had sprung up along the river.

"No," Diane said. "He was a loner. He never spoke of family or friends. He never spoke to the dogs or made friends here or made any effort to join in with other people. We had thought he might be an undercover Crule-in-training."

"They'd kill their own?" Matt asked.

"They wouldn't hesitate if it suited their purpose," Sandra said. "You've got a lot to learn about how ruthless these creatures are, Matt."

"Thanks for that," Matt said. He was getting fed up with being patronised all the time. Where was Lily when he needed her? She didn't patronise – she simply argued, which was much better. "So why would it suit their purpose to kill their own now? And what might Kevin have learnt that would benefit them if he really was an undercover Crule-in-training? Oh my Dog! The Crules know where we're going then," he stated flatly. "We must change our plans."

"No one knew," Diane said. "You didn't know where we were going. *'Need to know'* – remember? Kevin certainly didn't. Maybe they killed him to show other undercover Crules that they wouldn't tolerate less than perfect work."

"Do you mean there might be others amongst us?" Matt said looking around at their little group. "Can't you sniff them out?"

"Nope," Diane said.

"I didn't mean you. I meant Amber," Matt said huffily. Why had he ever thought she and he would make a good match?

"You shouldn't have said it aloud then," Diane said.

Trouble is, if they've already achieved lock-down I can't sense anything about them – they could be for us or against us or completely unaware of anything. I certainly hadn't sensed anything from Kevin the Hand. The ability to close down was always a protection for us, but now it can be used against us, unfortunately, and has become a double-ended-fang.

"There must be a way of making sure we're not taking any traitors into our new hiding place!"

"We could make everyone demonstrate communication with their dogs? Somehow," Sandra suggested. "But then, what about me, for example. I don't have a dog."

"Even then, someone could demonstrate it but we still won't know what that communication is – it could still be a Crule or a Crule-in-training whose dog is a Cur. How would we know the difference?"

We're in an exposed position right now, Amber prompted. *Let's get on.*

"What about the possibility of taking undercover Crules in with us?" Matt asked her.

Leave everyone behind but us. Come.

And Amber trotted up the path.

"What about Kevin?"

Leave him!

Matt couldn't bring himself to leave a corpse lying around on the path as though it was just another piece of litter. He dithered and looked beseechingly after Amber. He looked back at the corpse. If Kevin the Hand had been an old crisp bag or cigarette packet Matt would have picked him up and thrown him away in the right place. To simply leave him there went against everything he'd ever believed in.

At least until now…

The future of the Realm is at stake. Kevin the Hand was an enemy. I'm not losing more people for the sake of one enemy. Come! Bring your women. Leave the rest. If they are true to us they will understand and we will meet up later; if they are not then they will either protest and we will know for sure, or they will remain silent and be frustrated. Come!

Matt turned to Diane and Sandra now anxiously waiting to hear what was to happen. "We're to go with Amber. Just us three. The rest will understand. Get one of them to call the police about Kevin. His death will look like natural causes unless they have a way of measuring despair. But at least they will sort him out in terms of taking him away and giving him some kind of send-off."

A snort in his mind made him wonder if Hounds left their corpses around for the birds to pick.

We are Hounds. We dig a hole. We go back to the dirt.

Right. They go back to the dirt. Okay then. But humans tended to want something between their bodies and the dirt. Things like clean clothes and wooden caskets or at least cardboard or wicker baskets.

What for?

"Well, for… to… um… To stop us thinking about going back to the dirt, I suppose. I don't know."

Sounds like it just slows the process down. Can't see the point in that.

Diane went off and had a word with a man with wild hair, wearing three jumpers, and hugging a huge poodle. Sandra packed up their belongings scattered in the scuffle, and the three of them set off after Amber. When the others were lost to sight Amber came back to bring up the rear, and Diane took the lead. She was the only one who knew where they were going.

"It's not only that," she said. "But anyone who is with us is in danger. It's you and Amber they want – the rest of us are unimportant. So she's right to dump everyone anyway. It'll probably save their lives."

"What about you and Sandra, then?" Matt asked.

"We at least are more aware of the danger. The others," she waved her hand back down the trail. "They weren't, really. Not really. Maybe they are now, of course, but now they're probably thankful to be left behind. Unless they're undercover Crules of course."

"Won't they be following us?"

"Nah. I had a word with Ben. He's the one with the enormous poodle. He's one of ours. Definitely one of ours. He's going to make sure they all stay together so they can all watch each other. If anyone insists on leaving their group in the next six hours or so then we'll know who is a danger to us."

"How will you know?" Matt asked. "Do you communicate somehow with Ben? Or with his dog? Is his dog a Hound? I don't quite understand how these things work yet."

"Dog-dammit, Matt! He'll ring me!" and she pulled her mobile phone from the top pocket of her check shirt and waved it in his face in a really irritating manner. Matt clenched his jaws together.

"You ever heard of these things, Matt?" Diane went on. "Telephones. Mobile telephones. Mobile so you can move around with them and still make them work. Clever stuff. Ay?"

He could think of nothing to say that would flatten her so he tried to smile to show he shared the joke but all that happened was that his lips pulled back, baring his teeth, and she carried on up the path laughing in an unnecessarily uproarious way.

They trudged along. A breeze stirred itself and chilliness pervaded the air. Matt's ears were cold. The river reflected darkness only occasionally relieved by flashes of white in the sky. The water rolled along quietly, minding its own business. Matt wished everyone else would do the same. What had happened to his previously calm and uneventful life? He'd do anything to get that back. Warmth flooded his mind and he agreed with Amber that, actually, that wasn't true. Although uneasy about too many things now, he was glad he'd lived through the last few days. He only hoped he'd live through some more...

They passed a few people out for a walk; sounds of the city drifted down to them. Matt wondered how much longer they'd have to go on.

He caught up with Diane. She glanced at him over her shoulder, a supercilious grin appearing when she saw him.

"Do you mean you can't communicate with dogs?" he asked. Her grin disappeared to be replaced with a scowl.

"I'll take that as a no," he said and dropped back again.

He found himself strangely satisfied that he could communicate with Amber who could communicate with the poodle who could send information back to him, but Diane had to use a phone.

Not for long, though. A sharp brain nip and he was ashamed of his momentary smugness.

Pups will be pups, but if you'd been nicer you could have offered to do the communicating for her, but you were too busy being superior. Also, the only reason she can't communicate with dogs – **at the moment** *- is that she is a Compeer's descendant without a Hound to communicate with. You should be sympathetic, not puppishly unpleasant.*

"Well, she's not very nice to me is she?" he muttered. "It's the only time I've ever managed to feel superior. The rest of the time I've been on the floor!"

He could feel her softening; he could also feel her smiling. It made him smile too. He supposed he **was** still a pup in the grand scheme of things. That cheered him. He'd been feeling peculiarly old recently. Then he remembered Lily and a cloud of raging worry descended on him again.

Stop that! You mustn't allow yourself to be open to despair.

Immediately, he strengthened his thoughts. Lily would be fine. She was a survivor, that one, and she had Seb.

Diane stopped, and Matt looked up to see a large building in a state of advanced disrepair, what was left of it covered in mosses, lichen and ivy, trees reaching for the sky through the no-longer intact roof. His day-dreams of a comfortable bed, civilised washing facilities and yummy culinary arrangements disappeared.

"Come!" Diane said and marched forward. Inside the structure she led them on for ages. The building didn't seem big enough to be walking this long, but then she disappeared.

"Diane!" Matt raced forward only to find himself standing upright in a corridor next to her. She was fine. He was fine. He wasn't sure what had happened. What he did know was that he wouldn't be able to find this tunnel himself. Maybe that was the point. They must be underneath the ruins.

The others joined them and they set off once again. Their passage was lit by small, flickering lights set at uneven intervals in the walls. A few turnings later through a couple of heavy doors they came out into a bright, warm room of a fair size already occupied by a variety of people and dogs. They sat at tables and on benches, hot drinks in hand, a radio on low, and the remains of a meal on the big, dark-wood table. The chatter stopped as the new arrivals were spotted.

Everyone and their dog got up and stood, head bowed. Matt looked over his shoulder wondering who he'd see behind him before he realised they were showing respect to Amber. How could he have forgotten that she was royalty? Uncomfortably, he shifted from foot to foot, but Amber trod lightly into the room, and immediately lay down in the space that had appeared in front of the fire, whereupon everyone relaxed.

A man, tall and bearded with a dog that stood to his waist approached. "We've been looking forward to meeting you!" he said, holding his great shovel of a hand out to Matt who rather tentatively put his own in it and wondered if he'd ever get it back. "You must be Matt Lannings. I'm Todd Breen. This is Jenny," he said, turning to the dog. "Come and sit with us. Would you like tea or coffee? Something to eat?"

And the room erupted into chatter again as new conversations unfolded. Glancing over to the fire Matt saw Amber looking at him.

You're safe here. For now. Rest.

He turned back to Todd, grateful for the warmth of the mug thawing his freezing hands. He could relax, at least for a while.

Looking around as Todd went to get him a plate of the stew which smelled so amazing, Matt wondered if all these people were Compeers, or descendants of the Compeers exiled from the Realm. If not, who were they? And why did Amber trust them all?

"Yes, it's a great place, isn't it," someone was saying to Sandra. "It looks so abandoned on the outside, and of course, it is. It was a stone mill during the late nineteenth century for cutting and crushing stone from the quarries. No one would think to look beneath it. We've been using this place for decades, ever since the exile after the Great Betrayal. It was my ancestor in fact who made it so secure – he tunnelled it out and built the facilities down here. The mill's been in my family for centuries."

Matt finished his stew. It had been delicious. He'd have liked more but didn't have the nerve to ask for it. "Tell me more about this place, Todd. I'd like to know," he said.

"This is the headquarters for the Exiles and their offspring," Todd said. "Often, we need to disappear from society because Crules make life difficult so we stay here until we can fit back in again. But mostly, this is our HQ in the campaign to stop the increase of Crules-in-training. We try to convert them back to decency. I must admit, we don't have a very high conversion rate. But we try to prevent cruelty, bring down the puppy mills, the dog-fighting rings. Unbelievably, some of these things are legal in the Human Territories so we have to be careful."

Matt and Jenny followed Todd as he set off on his guided tour. "We try to spread the message that unkindness rots the mind. Watch your step there – the floor's a bit uneven." Matt watched his step.

"We've got a new problem now," Todd continued. "Hybrids. Crules have somehow abducted Hounds and bred them with dogs. The offspring are neither one thing nor the other; they are lost and distressed – rather like the offspring of the Compeers who have never been to the Realm, and don't understand why they don't quite fit in anywhere."

Todd shook his head, bewilderment alive on his face, as if, no matter how hard he tried, he simply could not comprehend how vile some humans could be.

Jenny shoved her broad head under Todd's arm, and Matt tried to look comforting, but didn't know what to say.

Todd went on: "There is a splinter group, youngsters in the main, who go much further and do wild things to rescue some dogs. They are generally disapproved of by most of us, but I fancy that at the same time most of us have a sneaking admiration for them."

They arrived back in the main room having toured through bedrooms, storerooms, healing rooms, more rooms than Matt would have thought possible down there.

Back where they started Matt was struck by a painting on the wall above the fireplace, and wondered why he'd not spotted it straight away. Now he had seen it, he couldn't stop looking at it. The picture was large, and framed in ornate gilt-edged wood. When people passed it they touched it – he wasn't even sure they were aware that they did so – just a light brushing of a hand along its frame or a quick tap of a finger on its edge. Some looked at it briefly in passing, but surely not long enough to actually *see* it. Everyone seemed aware that it was there and paid it some kind of attention.

Todd noted Matt's fascination. "Yes, that's our dream. It's called 'The Lost World'. It was painted by the Great Betrayer shortly after the Casting Out, before she disappeared." The big man's shoulders slumped. Jenny pushed her head into his hands and he wrapped them around her skull, fondling her ears and leaning his whole body forward as if more contact with her would mean less sadness out here. Then he shook himself, much like a dog would, and straightened up.

"Come and have a look," he invited Matt. "Despite being painted by the Great Betrayer, this is our pride and joy. This is the closest any of us have got to the Realm."

"Are there no original Exiles left?" Matt asked.

"No, I'm afraid not. None of them lived very long. It was as if they couldn't survive properly away from the Realm." They threaded their way between the tables. People leaned over and touched Matt's sleeve as he passed as though grounding themselves or as though they drew comfort from his presence. Matt thought they must be doing that as a way of getting closer to Amber.

Up close to the painting, Matt was overwhelmed with the longing it gave off. Every brush-stroke in this painting had come from a place of complete and utter love and the loneliness only known to those who've had that love, and lost it. Inside the somewhat ornate, hand-made frame, the outer edge of the picture was a threatening, jagged, almost scribbled, mix of purple, blues and greens in very dark shades, almost black; leading into the picture itself trees framed a sunlit view of open spaces, hills and fields of wildflowers.

And there was Amber! Matt craned forward to see better, his nose nearly touching the canvas. He inspected the dog minutely. Of course, it was a Hound, not a dog! And it *was* Amber. He looked enquiringly at Todd.

"To be honest, I don't know how it works – it is either your Hound or her ancestor. But I know that some of them can live for a very long time and word is that some of them live forever, however unlikely that might sound." He pinkened a little around his beard as though he felt uncomfortable saying anything so fantastical out loud.

"Don't worry. I've got used to getting used to things I never thought possible," Matt said, clapping him on the arm. "And I'm only a beginner at this."

Looking back at the picture, Matt could see that Amber, or her ancestor, stood within the arms of an achingly familiar woman with chestnut hair; another Hound, a great, black hairy beast who looked remarkably like Seb, stood just behind them as though proud of them, or as though he was on guard. Gazing at the tableau made by the two Hounds and the woman, all of them looking so sublimely happy, Matt felt a heat come to his eyes; he dashed tears away before they could fall. They looked complete, and yet, unbearably sad. A grief so powerful he'd never felt its like came over him and nearly buckled his legs.

Todd grasped Matt's arm and strength flowed back into him. He smiled gratefully in the big man's direction and pulled himself together, turning away from the picture. He couldn't bear to see it any more. Now he knew why no one really looked at it, but they all touched it. They wanted to be a part of it.

A sudden realisation dawned that explained why he was so powerfully moved by the picture – it was Lily. Of course – Lily! That's why the painted figure had been so familiar. Except it couldn't really be Lily. Could it?

Now she was back in his mind, all serenity fled. Was she okay? A query sent in Amber's direction produced a distinct shake of her head in his mind. No. There was no word from Seb.

Chapter Eleven

Lily's mouth felt as though a hamster had taken up residence having first lined it with sawdust. It must be the sleeping tablets. It felt like a battle had taken place in her brain, and bits of it were dying in agony inside her skull.

Groggily, she pulled herself upright and leaned back against the wall. Trying to looking around, she reckoned the occupant of the other bed must be fast asleep judging by the regularity of the heavy breathing. In fact, it was still dark and all she could see was a murky outline. What had woken her from such a deep, drugged sleep?

Me, me, me! It's me! Fer bones' sake, pull yourself together, pup!

Startled, Lily looked under the bed. There was nowhere else to look in this room. It only had two beds, two lockers and two chairs in it, nothing else. There was nowhere else for anyone to be.

Here, here, here. Window!

Sliding out of bed, trying not to make any noise, Lily went to the window and looked out. A very large dog stood there, its tail waving frantically to start with, but then it slowed and slowed, and finally drooped as she merely stared at it. It looked familiar. Did she have a dog? Was this her dog? She flattened her hand against the glass and the animal leapt forward and slammed into the window with such force she thought it would shatter. Startled, she stumbled backwards and fell over a chair. As she was falling to the floor, someone caught her and drew her upright. She was marched back to the window.

Looking out, she saw the dog was still there. Now, though, it curled back its lips to show the most fearsome array of teeth she'd ever seen in her life. Lily knew she should be afraid, but somehow she wasn't. The hand on her arm tightened and a not-so-pleasant breath wafted over her face. "Damn wild dogs! The place is getting overrun with them. I'll get onto the animal control officer to clear it out."

Lily. Lily. Lileeeeee....

She couldn't take her eyes off the dog. It must be her dog, surely. Or why would she feel so drawn to it? Why wasn't she frightened of it? She didn't like to think it would be mistreated. "They won't hurt it, will they?" she asked, looking over her shoulder and seeing Nurse Silver Lump on her mobile phone.

"No, of course not! We're not inhumane. Silly Billy." Nurse Silver Lump went back to the conversation she was having. Footsteps could be heard hurrying down the corridor, and Credence appeared in the doorway.

What was *he* doing here? He went straight to the window and when he looked out Lily could have sworn his own lips pulled back and an array of fangs just as impressive appeared, but surely not. It wasn't possible. As fast as it happened they were gone again. He turned to her, donning a reassuring smile, and approached.

"You can't be in here," Lily said. "This is a woman's ward." She glanced at the other bed hoping all the palaver hadn't woken her ward-mate, but there was no sign it had. Perhaps she was drugged up to the eyeballs as well.

"I was worried about you," he said. "You seemed so lost and alone and so very tired last night."

"It's still last night, isn't it?" she said, uncomfortable that she was only clad in a large t-shirt and her knickers. "You shouldn't be in here. Why have you been allowed in here?"

She didn't wait for an answer because the sound of vehicles approaching, the screeching of brakes, the sudden silence as engines were switched off, made her rush to the window.

Run, run, run, she screamed in her mind, directing her thoughts to the big dog outside. Run! She knew with utter certainty that they **would** be inhumane if they caught him. She felt active hostility flowing from this room outwards. Lily looked at Credence and could see nothing but hatred, which in this moment was directed solely at that poor, defenceless animal out there, who'd never do anyone any harm, she knew it.

Heck, heck, heck.

And in an instant love surrounded her, lifted her, strengthened her, and she knew it was Seb, her Hound, her Compeer, and they meant to kill him. "Run!" she screamed. "Run!"

"There. I told you. She's relapsing. She needs it now."

And once again, she was on the floor, several people holding her down even though she wasn't struggling, and once again, she was injected with some concoction that blanked her mind out.

But not before she realised who she was, and who Seb was, and that he had risked everything and dropped his guard for her to give her something worth more than life itself. She felt a burst of early morning sun on her face, the wind racing through her hair, her muscles contracting and releasing, and she was flying, flying through the air, over the fence, her paws hitting the ground, and the ecstasy that was freedom and friendship and joy shot through her and made her laugh. She was free. Seb was free. As she fell into the enemy's darkness, represented by Credence's gargoylesque scowl, she took Seb's offering of golden light with her, firmly embedded in her mind. Nothing could make her lose it again. Nothing.

When she woke next, her mouth was too stiff and dry to use. This time it was full daylight, so a few hours must have passed. She drank the entire jug of water on her bedside locker and stuffed several mint humbugs into her mouth. Harder to deal with was the leaden weight in her limbs and her head was so heavy she couldn't work out how she was managing to hold it up. She let it fall to rest on her chest and looked in the mirror. She had to peer at herself from the side in order to see anything. It wasn't a good look. Forcing herself erect again she staggered from the room and out into the corridor. It was very quiet out there. She didn't even know what time of day it was.

Shambling back into her room she got dressed. Cautiously advancing down the corridor towards the communal areas, she could see everyone outside in the garden. She hadn't thought the weather nice enough to hang about out there, but decided to join them in case there was something going on she should know about.

Lily walked through the dining area and slid the doors to the garden open. Stepping out onto the patio she could see across the fields to the trees at the foot of the hill. They looked so far away. They looked too far for her to ever imagine she could sit in their shade.

People were clustered around the biggest wooden table, some smoking, some not. This wasn't about smoking outside. This was a gathering of some kind. Some sat on the big swing seat and some on the ground. She looked around for Delilah. She'd given up thinking of her as her mother – it didn't compute. There was absolutely nothing there, no spark of affection, not even the pull of liking that sometimes you get when you first meet someone. About to decide that Delilah must be in her room or maybe on some course where you could finger paint, or learn how to bake a potato, Lily spotted her kneeling by the fence, her face pressed up against it. What *was* she doing? Getting closer, Lily could see there was a ragged crack in the wood. Delilah was forcing it open in order to peer through. Of course, she was too short to see over the fence.

The people sitting down must have given up trying to see – there were too many other, taller people, already straining to see over the fence. Or maybe whatever they'd been watching had finished now. Idly, she wondered what it was that had interested them all so much, but there didn't appear to be anything to see now so she might as well go back to bed. She still felt very weary and she didn't fancy bumping into Credence. There was something very strange and menacing about him. She didn't like feeling menaced.

Turning to go back inside, a shout went up behind her. Startled, she hesitated, but something made her turn. By this time the ranks of people at the fence had thickened; Delilah was completely hidden by people's legs behind her; others were pushing and shoving trying to get a view. Those previously sitting had clambered up onto the tables so they could see. A sudden searing urgency made Lily grab a man in passing. "What's everyone looking at?" she demanded.

"Where've you been all morning?" he said and looked her up and down as though she were a strip of wallpaper he was measuring with his eyes. He pulled away, but Lily tightened her hand on his arm. A ferocity so alien to her she frightened herself rushed out of her mouth: "I asked you a question," she hissed. "What's everyone looking at?"

Bones! She frightened herself.

"All right. All right. Keep yer hair on!" he said, looking considerably less confident. "It's a wolf if you must know. They've been chasing a wolf for hours out there."

"A wolf?" She let him go. He made off with great speed. A wolf? But wolves had been extinct in England for the last five hundred years. Maybe one had escaped from a local zoo. Whatever it was wouldn't make any difference to her, and she didn't want to stick around to see it caught and no doubt badly treated through no fault of its own. She headed for the sliding doors.

Wolf! Heck! Like a mere wolf could have outwitted them all this morning waiting for you to wake up! What a sluggard. What a sluggardly pup! Heck, heck, heck.

A roar went up from the audience and Lily jumped onto the table nearest her. She could see a couple of motorbikes racing across the field. A 4x4 bounced along behind them. Various other people were running around aimlessly waving sticks. The motorbikes looked awfully close to the running figure she could see flickering through the undergrowth. She stopped breathing. Some fireworks went off. Fireworks?

Oops. He thought he had me then. I'll just bounce around a bit. Give him some hope. This would make a great painting, Lily. You could call it, 'Bouncing through the bullets'. Poor thing. He's going to be so disappointed when he misses me again.

It was only then Lily realised the sticks were guns. They were shooting at the wolf!

You're not awake yet. Wake up, Lily! Wake up!

Lily looked around to see who was talking to her. As she did so, she caught sight of Credence. He scowled fiercely at her and a strike of golden lightning hit her and released her from the dark again.

Seb! Lily shrieked in her head. Get out! I'm awake. Thank you! I have you. I won't forget you again. Credence is my prompt, you clever Hound, you! Go! Go! I can't bear it. I couldn't bear it if they got you.

Right you are. I'm off. See you later.

Of course, Credence knew she and Seb were broadcasting. He strode over to her and stood far too close, but she wasn't afraid any more. She had Seb back, she wouldn't lose him again, and with Seb behind her she could do anything. They stared at each other for a long time. She had to admit – Credence was scary!

"What are you doing, Credence?" Both Lily and Credence flinched at the voice. It was like a whip crack. Lily was surprised to see her mother. She hadn't thought Delilah could be forceful. She'd seemed like such a poor dab of a thing.

Credence stepped away from Lily. "Nothing, Del. We were just talking about the wolf, weren't we, Lily?"

Why was he backing down from his wife? He didn't seem the sort to ever back down from anyone.

"You have to watch him," Delilah said to Lily. "He likes younger women." She shot Credence a very strange look. What an odd thing for Delilah to say to her! Was she warning her away from her husband, or her husband away from her?

Credence gave Delilah a meaningful look and she answered it with a frown.

What was going on between these two? Lily didn't want to know, except that she **did** want to know because she was sure it had something to do with her.

She let them get on with their frowning wars while she hugged Seb's golden light to herself. For at least as long as she could see Credence, especially if he scowled, which was pretty often, he would remind her of that Seb-given light – and it was when he was around that she needed the reminder most. The rest of the time she was certain of Seb anyway. He was a real genius, that Hound.

A 'heck' echoed in her mind, only it sounded far away now. Thankfully.

"Why don't you stay here and have a game of crib with someone," Delilah said to Credence. "Let me and Lily get to know one another. It's about time." She nodded her head at Credence and he went off as though he always obeyed her when she spoke to him. It was such an odd view of him after all the menace.

Lily looked after him as he joined a crowd at the table. They moved up the moment they saw him coming. He did have an indefinable air of menacing authority about him.

"Come, Lily." Delilah took her arm and headed for the patio doors. "Let's get comfortable in my rooms, get some peace away from everyone else. Have a cup of tea, maybe." She wasn't taking no for an answer. Lily would have had to make a huge fuss to avoid going with her.

Lily was virtually frog-marched down the corridor, down another corridor, and another until they seemed to be miles from everyone else, and then a couple of lefts and a right, and a seriously substantial door later, and they entered a room so unlike the rooms Lily had so far seen that she wondered if they'd left the hospital altogether. She stared around at the solid wood furniture, lush upholstery and curtains, pictures on the wall in great, gilt frames, flowers on the tables, an enormous aspidistra in its jardinière, an artistic display of fruit in a lovely hand-painted ceramic bowl.

Delilah went straight to the sideboard and switched on a coffee machine. "What would you like?" she asked, finding a cup and placing it on the cup stand. She ran her finger along a row of boxes containing coffees and teas.

Wow. This looked like half-decent coffee. "I'll have an Americano, please. That would be lovely," Lily said.

"Do sit down."

Lily couldn't decide between the chaise longue and the rocker chair. Who wanted to sit on an armchair when there were more exotic forms of seating available? She settled on the chaise in the end, thinking it was more sociable than a seat that would be in constant motion if she sat in it. And who could sit in a rocking chair without rocking it? And drink coffee. Okay. Chaise, it was.

Delilah removed the steaming cup and put another under the nozzly thing, chose a pod from its box and set the machine whishing and gurgling again. She brought the first cup to Lily.

In comparison with what she'd had in the last few days this coffee was nectar! It cleared any remaining traces of fog from her brain, too. "Thank you so much. Forgive me for asking, but how come your accommodation is like this when the rest of the place is more like a hospital?"

"Although attached, it's not part of The Haven," Delilah said, heading for the door and making sure it was properly closed. She checked a box on the wall and switched something with an audible click.

"Have you just switched on an alarm? Why've you done that with us inside?"

"I'm making sure we can be ourselves without anyone detecting us should we accidentally broadcast, but especially so that Credence doesn't. This house is now guarded so we can talk properly."

Lily's attention had been caught, however, by a large painting on the wall above an open fireplace. There was no fire, but the room was still warm. The fireplace was big enough to roast a very large cow and Lily thought it must be for decoration, or maybe it would be lit on cold winter evenings. It had a solid slate surround within which were what looked like genuine antique tiles depicting fields riotous with flowers. In the hearth was an enormous arrangement of bulrushes and dried grasses enlivened by several colourful king protea flowers, all tastefully arranged in an old brass coal scuttle.

The painting, which on closer inspection turned out to be a print, was a blue-skied, lushly bright landscape with a very dark, jagged edging suggestive of threat. In the foreground Seb, looking even hairier than usual, stood guard over herself and Caramel Girl.

How could this be possible? Lily got even closer and realised it was an older version of herself with longer hair. Was this a picture of the future? And why would she be hugging Caramel Girl rather than Seb?

The picture pulled at her; it made her want to cry.

"Ah, you've spotted 'The Lost World,'" Delilah said, joining her at the fireplace, her coffee cupped in her hands as though she were cold. "My mother painted that when she was grieving. Not that she ever stopped grieving, of course, but this was soon after the Casting Out. You can feel the sorrow coming off it, can't you? It was one of the few ways she could genuinely express herself, her painting, without giving herself away to Credence and his followers. I believe you've inherited the gift. It passed me by completely I'm afraid."

"This was painted by my grandmother? Was it my grandmother? Are you my birth mother?" Lily asked, running her hand down the frame as if needing the contact.

"You know the answer to that already, Lily. Yes, I am your birth mother. Yes, this picture was painted by your grandmother."

Lily felt no surprise but she couldn't bring herself to look at Delilah. "It's difficult to imagine my grandmother," she said. "I wish I'd known her."

"That is her in the picture," Delilah said. "You look just like her."

"Why is it called the 'The Lost World'?"

"Because it depicts the Realm and the Hounds and the loss of both."

"My grandmother was a Compeer?"

Delilah hesitated and looked down. Before she could answer, Lily had rushed on: "This is a print," she said. "Where's the original? Did she sell her work?"

"No. Well, yes, she did sell her work. That's how they made a living to begin with. But she'd never have sold the original to this piece. It hangs in the Exiles' headquarters."

"The Exiles' headquarters," Lily repeated. "What do you mean?"

"Okay, Lily. We need to cover a lot of ground and we don't have much time." Delilah pulled her to the chaise and they sat on it close together as though they were going to share secrets.

"Now concentrate," her mother admonished. "You've got to take this in quickly and quietly. Thanks to you and your friends there's even less time than I thought we had. Not that I mind. The waiting is the worst. Are you listening?"

Lily nodded, no clue as to what was coming next, no clue at all.

"The original of that painting hangs in the Exiles' HQ because Anne, my mother, your grandmother, otherwise known as the Great Betrayer, painted it to provide a focus for our efforts, an image of what we were striving to preserve, even if we could never get back to it."

Lily felt sure she'd heard incorrectly. This woman, her mother, was saying Lily was the granddaughter of the Great Betrayer, the woman who risked the safety of the Realm for an infatuation, and got the Compeers thrown into exile forever.

If this were true, Seb would never forgive her, because that meant her grandmother got his grandsire murdered, not to mention Seb also felt his family had betrayed the Realm by letting the Great Betrayer go free. So he would feel guilty *and* vengeful.

But it couldn't be true. How could it be true?

"Concentrate," Delilah said again, tugging on her arm. "There's not much time. Credence is your grandfather, the Great Betrayer's mate. He is my father, not my husband. We lie to the world that we are man and wife so people can make silly jokes about the age difference – they're so busy doing that they never wonder who he really is. They know who I am," she said, bitterness leaching into her voice. "They know I'm the Great Betrayer's daughter. But they don't know who he is. I keep him hidden, if you like. I keep him hidden from the Exiles and their descendants so that they're also hidden from him. This also gives me cover, and he has no idea."

Lily wondered if her mouth was hanging open. She looked around as if to make sure she hadn't fallen down a rabbit hole. Maybe more drugs had been slipped her way than she'd thought.

"Come on! Listen to me," Delilah snapped. "Apart from that one awful mistake, your grandmother protected the Realm her whole life even though she knew she'd never see it again, and she taught me to do the same. You're the one, Lily, who makes all the sacrifices worthwhile. You're the one who will cause the Compeers and their descendants to go back to the Realm. You're the One Who Knows Not Who You Are. Until now."

That explained that fragment then! It only had the essential bit missing from it, that was all!

"Your grandmother organised the rebels and I found out. It meant I couldn't go home to my husband and my daughter. My baby daughter. I had to choose between service to the Realm, a place I'd never seen and never would see, and my love for my daughter. I had to do what I had to do. I wasn't able to do what I wanted to do." The longing on her face was so naked and raw Lily wanted to cry, but it was too late; too late for her to give her mother a hug or say anything useful. Her mother had chosen the Realm and Lily grew up thinking someone else was her mother. She couldn't change how she felt about that.

Delilah coughed and blew her nose. "Reconciliation is the key," she went on. "And it can only be gained after acknowledgement of the great ill that has been perpetrated against both sides. Only then can forgiveness be given. And only then can reconciliation be achieved. This is why some very particular circumstances had to be brought to pass before the Compeers could go home and the Realm could be saved. So the Great Betrayer, or her representative, has to be here. And she has to be forgiven by the Greatest Betrayed of them all and that is her Hound, or his descendant, and we need the Supremity to represent the Realm. She has to be forgiven for the Casting Out, for the great ill done the Compeers. I believe she's here in the Human Territories at the moment."

Lily kept a straight face. She didn't want to give anything away in case this was all a trick.

"And then the way is clear for Compeers to go back to the Realm. And although I had a wobble after my mother, Anne, died, I'm now ready to deal with my father, Credence, to prevent him from sabotaging the Great Return."

"Deal with him?"

"You can't kill Crules. They can only be made ineffectual somehow. I couldn't kill him anyway. He's my father and no matter what else he is, I love him."

"How will you do it?" Lily asked. "He's large and powerful, and you're... uh... not so much..."

Delilah smiled sadly. "I'll have surprise on my side. He won't expect me to betray him. I can't tell you details or you might accidentally give me away. Suffice to say that he has to be stopped. Because of the peculiar circumstances, the Path of Valediction will open and Credence and his followers will be ready to get back to the Realm. This time, the Realm wouldn't survive the onslaught. They mustn't be allowed to get there."

Lily was still reeling from the knowledge that she was directly related to the Great Betrayer. She drained her cup and stared into it, wishing it would fill itself with strong coffee. How could she possibly be the Great Betrayer's granddaughter? "Can't we sort all this out once we're in the Realm?" she queried, looking hopefully up at her mother.

"When you say 'we', I don't think you can go."

"Not go to the Realm?" Lily gasped. Delilah might as well have punched her in the stomach. "I've got to go to the Realm. Seb's my Hound. I'm Seb's Compeer. I can't be apart from him. I'll die."

"A tad melodramatic, don't you think? You'll survive. Your grandmother had to after her Hound was murdered."

"But she was the Great Betrayer. It served her right!"

"She had a moment of weakness over a man. Of course, you'd never put a foot wrong, would you!" Delilah snapped. "After all you know about her now, all the sacrifices, all the risks and bravery involved in setting up the Exiles' movement and HQ, you still call her that!"

Lily remained mute. She couldn't take in the idea of never seeing Seb again. Or Caramel Girl. But mainly Seb. Never see the Realm. What had all this been about if she were to lose what she'd only just gained?

"I have to go to the Realm. Why can't I go?" Lily had to squeeze the words around the boulder that had appeared in her throat.

"You're too emotional. You wouldn't make it over the Path. The Void would get you. Also, someone has to be here. There are thousands of Crules-in-training now, thousands of Curs, Dog knows how many Hound hybrids. All these creatures need someone they can turn to, the Realm needs someone here to ward off the worst dangers and warn them of potential ones. Someone has to fight it. Someone has to head up the rebel cause. That someone has to be you. I'm sorry."

"Why can't it be you?" Lily whispered, anguish spreading through her like boiling venom in her veins. "Why does it have to be me?"

"I won't be here," Delilah said. "Wait!" she added as Lily opened her mouth to answer. Delilah held up a hand for silence, and tilted her head as though listening.

Lily listened too, but could hear nothing.

"The Crules are collecting," Delilah said. "We must go. I to Credence, you to re-join Seb and the others."

"How do I do that?"

Delilah pointed to the painting. "Climb in to the fireplace, go around the dried flower arrangement, through the gap in the wall behind it. It's small but it was made for people of our build – that is, Anne and me and you. Wriggle along there for a bit and you'll come out at the back of this part of the building into a brick-built lean-to type shed. We put a washing machine, tumble dryer, and other laundry stuff in there to make anyone lose interest should they look in."

Delilah glanced at the door, her eyes widened as if she'd heard something worrying, and when she spoke again, her words fell over each other in their haste to be said: "I will have pushed the tumble dryer back into place last time, so when you come out of the tunnel you will have to move that out of the way. Then you'll be in the utility room. You come out of the back door of that, carefully. Keep an eye out in case there's anyone loitering around there although I can't think why there would be. Run across the gap – it's very small – and you'll be in the trees."

Delilah pulled Lily up from her seat and pushed her towards the fireplace. "Carry on up the hill and you'll see an old fallen-down wall. On the other side of that the land slopes down towards the river. By that time I expect Seb will have found you. But if not, carry on down the hill in the direction of the river and on your left you'll see a very large old mill that's fallen into major disrepair, trees growing up through it and all sorts. Underneath that is the rebels' HQ." Her words had got faster and faster until they tripped over themselves.

"Wait, wait…" Lily said.

"No, I can't. Something's going on. I've got to get out there before Credence wants to know where I am and comes looking for me. You've got to go." Delilah pushed her forward again.

"But…"

"There's no time for buts!" Lily was in the fireplace now. A spiky protea flower caught in her hair and she yanked it away. "Go. Go," Delilah cried. Tears streamed down her face and she kept her head down as if doing so would make sure Lily didn't notice them.

"Wait! When will I see you again?" Lily asked, snatching at her mother's hands and holding them still.

"I don't know. I don't know. You've got to go. Look at me – I've lost control of my emotions. Credence will know. I'm so sorry. You won't have the head start you should have had, but I don't know when I will see you again."

"I thought the place was guarded against transmitting emotions."

"It is. But even the best guard won't completely blank out extreme emotions."

"Extreme?"

"I might never see you again," Delilah explained, her voice breaking even as she managed to get her tears in check, and transform her face back to its usual impassive mask. "I would have liked to have known you better. I've watched over you for years, but I don't really know you."

Lily couldn't speak. She knew she would lose all control if she did. She stood there staring at her mother, knowing that if she opened her mouth she would simply howl her head off. She held out her arms and her mother walked into them as though they'd been exchanging hugs her entire life.

"But I do know you're a fine young woman and I'm very, very proud of you," Delilah said. She stood back, once more in command of herself. "I must go now before Credence finds us. You go. Be safe."

Lily gave her one more quick hug and a peck on the cheek and without looking back stepped into the fireplace avoiding the spiky flower this time and squeezed through the crack in the back wall. It was dark in there. She heard the flower arrangement being shifted back and forth as Delilah put it back in its proper place. Lily gulped in a few deep lungfuls of air to keep her incipient sobs in check and forced herself on until she smacked her head on something metallic and hoped she'd arrived at the tumble dryer. Relieved she didn't have to shuffle any further through such a confined space, she gently pushed at the dryer until there was room enough for her to sidle out of the tunnel and around the side of the machine, which she then replaced.

She was glad to see the light, although it was dim because the window was small and filthy. As she stood there trying to hear if anything was going on outside the lean-to, it came to her with a very bad feeling, that Delilah hadn't actually said how she was going to prevent Credence from getting back into the Realm. A premonition about the whole business sat in the bottom of her chest like an anchor.

Nothing could be heard from the other side of the door, no matter how much she strained her ears, so she pulled it open and looked around. All she could see were gently waving grasses, old thistles and a few ragged yellow flowers. This part of The Haven's grounds obviously didn't get mown she was pleased to see. She darted across to the copse and tripped over a large, furry Hound lying in wait for her. Before she could haul herself to her feet Seb pounced on her and licked her face raw.

See! Can't let you out on your own, young pup, can I? Always getting in trouble if I'm not around. You're enough to give me grey hairs. Heck, heck.

Lily finally managed to get her arms around him and ducked her face into his chest. What a relief to stop the licking while she still had some features left on her head. She could feel his heart thumping against her cheek. It was so good to be home. She burst into tears.

Oy! What's all this. You're supposed to be pleased to see me!

"I *am* pleased to see you," she sobbed. "That's why I'm crying."

Humans! Who can understand them?

Lily remembered she shouldn't be broadcasting and looked wildly around to see if the enemy had surrounded them yet after her ill-conceived outburst.

Yep. We're surrounded. Crules-in-training and Curs everywhere.

"Oh, no!"

What did you expect with all that emoting all over the place? Bound to happen.

"Emoting?"

Good word innit? Got that from Diane. Emoting. Stop emoting. Oy! Keep the emoting down.

"It's not funny if we're surrounded, you know."

No. Not funny. Wrong word. A trifle amusing.

"A trifle amusing?"

Yep.

He grabbed her by the back of her jacket and threw her in the air. While she flew, trying really hard not to scream, he edged himself around to be directly under her as she fell. She whumped down onto his back. He appeared to have grown bigger again, like he did last time she'd used him for transport. She clung onto his neck, her face pressed hard against his fur. He smelled of biscuits and sausages.

Sausages! Yay for sausages!

And he thundered along for a bit before an especially large lunge and contraction of all his muscles made him go into warp speed. Lily shut her eyes. She didn't want to see the ground whizzing past; she just wanted to be a part of Seb. She clung on harder. She never wanted to let him go. When her mind wandered to the subject of their approaching separation, she brought the shutters down to guard herself against the anguish, and to stop Seb picking up on it. Or did he know? Did he know they must soon part? Stop it Lily! She went blank.

When she did open her eyes again he'd reduced his speed to a canter and they were nowhere near where she expected to be. They were on the Downs overlooking the city, miles away from the rebels' HQ. Aghast, she gazed at the expanse of green all around them except on the side that looked down into the Avon gorge.

Maybe they were meeting someone here?

No, but we had to go in the opposite direction to the one we wanted or we'd have led the Crules straight to the rebels. So here we are.

There was no one in sight, no other creatures apart from a lone seagull floating on the currents above the gorge.

Also, I wanted a few minutes with you alone, young pup.

He sounded more serious than she'd ever heard him and she leaned against his side, her arm over his neck.

The Crules and Curs think they are still following us – we led them on, but a group of some of the rebels who don't want to go to the Realm, and some of the hybrid mutts, are now leading them even further away. So, we only have a short while, but I wanted you alone because I need to tell you that you're not coming back with us. Seb's head dropped until his nose nearly touched the grass, as though it was suddenly too heavy to hold up.

Lily couldn't stop herself this time. She sobbed into his neck, hardly able to draw breath. This was worse than anything she'd ever felt before, even though she'd had some warning.

"It's because of all the descendants who want to stay here, and all the hybrids," she said. "I know. It's my duty to stay and look after them."

*To hell with that! That's only something you would do if you choose. It's not something I would ask of you. Who told you that? Ah! Your mother. Poor Delilah. So bound up in taking on the responsibilities of **her** mother. Trying so hard to make up for the Great Betrayer.*

"You know?"

Yes, indeedy, and Caramel Girl knows. We know it all now. So much has come clear for us.

"But, you know that I am the Great Betrayer's granddaughter?"

Yes, but I have forgiven her. She spent the rest of her life trying to make up for it, and her daughter is doing the same, and in doing so she lost her family – that is – you, but enough's enough. I don't want you to sacrifice yourself, too. I have forgiven my Grandsire for letting her go when he should have killed her. My love for you has taught me what that bond really means. Oh, and my love for Caramel Girl has taught me a thing or two as well...

Lily gave him an 'I told you so' look.

Yeah, yeah. You were right. My love for her has taught me something of what Anne might have felt for her mate. And I know from Anne and Delilah's actions that they've forgiven the Realm for the Casting Out. So, we're all set to regain our balance, make ourselves complete. As long as we can escape Credence and his legions, that is...

He added the last bit almost under his breath. Lily ignored it. "But – without me? How can I ever be complete without you?"

You will learn. As I have to learn to live without you, young pup.

"No! That's not fair! You've just been going on about me not sacrificing myself and yet now you're saying I must. How can I live here without you? To hell with the Realm! To hell with the bloody Exiles, the bloody stupid Crules, the bloody, bloody…" Lily burst into wild tears and stomped around gabbling incoherently. She didn't know what to do with herself. She wanted to kill someone. She wanted to kill herself. She wanted to scream and make walls fall down until things went the way they should. She didn't know what she wanted apart from never to be separated from Seb.

This is why you can't go. Not all the other reasons Delilah might have given you, but because you're not trained, you're not disciplined, you can't be unfeeling enough at will. You're like a bumbling puppy. You emote at a change in the breeze. You'd never get over the Path. I can't let you take the risk. I had no idea when I first came here that you would turn out to be so untrained given your early life, but it's like you've only just hit your middle young years and you're rebelling against everything in sight. Which is good in some ways, but won't work for you on the Path. Matt might just about be able to manage it, but you won't. And I can't let you try. You must stay here and live your life, be happy and have lots of pups, and paint lots of pictures. What about this one?

And he struck a noble pose, head pulled back, lots of ruffled chest to the fore, paws firmly planted on the ground, tail carefully arranged in a curl, a twinkle of hope in his eyes, and a small smile on his face.

Lily burst into tears again.

See. Exactly my point.

But she looked up at him as his voice in her head had faded a little at the end, and she saw a silvery trace of fluid escape his eyes and run straight down his nose. He tried very hard to look blank but the drips off the end of his muzzle told another story. His anguish escaped him finally and he lifted his head and howled at the sky. Just once. Then he shook himself viciously until the ground trembled beneath his paws and he eyed her sternly: *I can't lose you.*

"No! I can't lose *you*!" she wailed. "I can't live without you now. Why did you ever come here if I was only going to lose you?"

We had to connect to make things right. Your family, the Realm itself in the person of Caramel Girl, and my family were the ones that needed reconciliation to make things healthy again. I'm sorry but I can't imagine life now without ever having known you. There'd be this huge gap in it, and I'd be a lesser Hound because of it. I'm glad I had to come here.

"Now I understand the unfeeling way," Lily mumbled. "It is so much better not to feel anything in the first place, not to get attached to anyone, not to love anyone, not to take the risk. The cost of losing them is too awful to be borne."

Without me you'd never have met Matt, Seb offered as if knowing that Rude Git Matt Lannings could ever make up for never seeing Seb again, never have him laugh in her mind, never experience his relish at finding a new word, never have him pose for a particularly appealing picture again.

"Matt!" she exclaimed, barely refraining from snorting.

If not for Caramel Girl and my duty to the Realm I would stay here to be with you.

Lily pulled herself together. "You couldn't do that. You would fade away and die without the Realm. I know that. At least I've never been there so I won't miss it like my grandmother did."

I would, however, fade away and die if you got lost in the Void.

"All right. I understand. I'm to stay here. But just tell me how I can possibly manage without you, having had you in my life, even if only for such a short time."

I will send you a gift.

"A gift?" She hadn't expected him to say that. What could he possibly send her from the Realm? She was pretty certain he couldn't pick up a phone and have flowers delivered.

You will know it when you see it. I'm not sure when it will appear, but appear it will. You must treasure it.

"I will!" And against all logic she felt better to think that at some unknowable point in the future there would be a tangible sign that Seb still thought of her.

The time has come. We must go now. This is farewell Lily, cherished pup. Whatever happens, do not step foot on the Path, and do not believe what you see on the Path.

She hugged him again and stood looking noble herself, chest out, shoulders back, head up, trying very hard to look fearless and determined. She was doing her Queen Boudicca thing. All she needed was a spear and a horse-drawn fighting chariot.

Stop that! Honestly, melodramatic to the end. Hop on. We've got to get to the mill. You don't happen to have any sausages on you, do you? He looked hopeful.

She ignored him, leapt onto his back, and Seb immediately took off. "Where does the Path of Valediction start, then?" she asked.

I'm not sure. It appears in response to the right person being at both ends of it. It has to be someone who can do it, like Caramel Girl or an Ageless One or a full-blown Crule, like Credence.

"You mean it comes into existence then?"

No. It is always in existence, but not always accessible. It has to be there all the time for the other worlds as well as ours.

"There are other worlds?"

Of course there are!

"I'm new to all this. Why should I necessarily know that?"

It's a bit arrogant to think we are the only creatures who have formed a world where we live and that we might want to leave from time to time.

"Okay."

And abruptly, they'd arrived. The Path was there. Even never having seen it before, Lily knew it could be nothing other than the Path of Valediction stretching out before her, brilliantly lit along its length as far as she could see, the swirling darkness of the Void abutting it on both sides; wisps of it seemingly reaching up to grasp at the unwary.

Farewell, cherished pup. Do not step foot on the Path. Do not believe what you see.

And he was gone. Her Seb Hound was gone. He was half-way down the Path and Lily couldn't understand how he'd got so far without her noticing.

It wasn't just Seb on the Path. Amongst several struggling knots of people, Lily could see Matt being punched repeatedly by a creature so wreathed in grey it was hard to make out its shape. While she watched, a Cur ran at Matt and sank its fangs in to his leg. He bellowed and went down, only to struggle back up again, hitting out and yelling, the utter fury in his voice clearly giving him the will to go on.

And there was Credence, striding past Matt's battleground, Delilah by his side, running to keep up! Oh, no! He was already on the Path! Delilah's plan to prevent him gaining the Path must have failed. Now what? The only hope was that there were enough Compeers to stop him actually getting in to the Realm on the other side of the Path.

Lily's attention was distracted by a heaving mess of people and Curs falling onto the Path, and a woman – it looked like Diane – slipped through the melee and raced away into the distance.

Many more were prevented from gaining access to the Path by a thin line of people and dogs stretched across it, protecting it. Lily ran to help. The Crules had to be stopped from entering the Realm! Credence's backup must be stopped!

She raced into the nearest screaming mass of bodies. She got fleeting glimpses of Mellow and Yellow, and a big man with an enormous poodle glued to his side, fighting off a crushing onslaught of Curs, a howling dankness egging them on, and she gritted her teeth, thought of Seb, and kicked out for all she was worth, her fists windmilling furiously, not knowing if she was having any effect at all.

Except that there was a sudden silence in which a wavering cry shredded the air. Lily's gaze was drawn to the Path in time to see Delilah, her arm entwined in Credence's, fall over the side into the grasping reaches of the Void below.

Delilah!

But a screaming howl, obviously Seb's, ripped her attention, and her breath, away from her mother's fate; acid horror flooded Lily's mouth; she looked for Seb, and saw his head jerk up as if he'd received a mortal wound to his chest; he stumbled to the edge of the Path and hurled himself into the Void. She could see his body flying through the air and falling out of sight into the darkness.

"No!" she shrieked and raced to the start of the Path. She would get him back. There must be a way! It couldn't end like this! But something prevented her. Someone held her back and dragged her away. She kicked and yelled, but couldn't move, and all this time Seb was falling further and further into the Void and an eternal life that wasn't life. And she couldn't even go after him. He would be lost and alone and would never know that she wanted to go with him.

"No!" Matt shouted. "No, Lily!" And he pulled her away from the edge of the Path. By this time others were helping and many hands helped to pull her struggling body from the danger zone. She screamed and cursed and hit out at them. And then she went blank.

When consciousness returned, she stared around trying to work out where she was. She was in the woods near the mill.

The Path was gone.

And Seb was in the Void of Nothingness.

"Seb!" she cried, sobs shuddering through her body. She threw herself on her face and clawed at the earth as if she could dig her way through to the Void.

"Lily," Matt's mouth was close to her ear. He knelt down, one hand on the ground to support himself, the other on her back. He said it again: "Lily – Seb is fine. That wasn't Seb. Seb is fine. That wasn't Seb. Seb is fine. That wasn't Seb."

When the words he was saying got through to her she forced herself to turn over and look up at him. She could see the branches swaying in the breeze behind his head, against a sky so blue and peaceful.

"That wasn't Seb? It looked like Seb. Why wouldn't you let me go to him? If it wasn't Seb, who was it?"

"It was the Void making you think it was Seb. That's what it does. It wanted you to think that and it got you immediately because you were wide open to it. Luckily we were all there and stopped you from doing what it wanted." He looked at the crowd of people hovering anxiously around them.

"That wasn't Seb?" she asked.

"No."

"You're certain it wasn't Seb?"

"It definitely wasn't Seb. It was the Void making you believe it was Seb. No Hounds went over the edge. None."

"It definitely wasn't Seb?"

"Definitely wasn't Seb."

She heaved herself over again, threw herself to the ground and burst into tears. She heard Matt say: "For Pete's sake! What do I have to do to make her believe me?"

And she heard Sandra say: "She does believe you, Matt."

"Then why's she crying now?" he demanded in rising tones of frustration.

"Because she does believe you, Matt."

"Aarghh!" and he stomped off.

Sandra helped her to sit up and produced a tissue. Lily scrubbed her face with it but she'd never feel better again. Seb was gone. Gone for good and it was like he'd taken all her insides with him. She was just a husk of herself. It was amazing her outer skin didn't collapse in on itself because there was nothing left inside to stop it from doing so. She'd probably wrinkle up like an old sultana now with nothing to keep her skin pushed out. Still, at least it would make it easy to keep her guard up. She never wanted to hurt like this again. She would spend the rest of her life practising and perfecting the unfeeling way.

"He did say he'd send a gift, which might help," Sandra said gently.

Lily's mouth twisted and she couldn't speak for fear of breaking down again. She merely nodded.

"He told me," Sandra said. "So that I could keep reminding you to look out for it. He thought it might pitch up in about four months or so. Time passes differently in the Realm. He asked me if I'd keep an eye on you at least until then. So I hope you don't mind, but I did say I would."

Lily nodded again. What difference did it make? She didn't care any more anyway.

"Come on – let's get you a drink." Sandra pulled Lily to a standing position and set off towards the mill. There were sporadic outbursts of fighting and cursing but nothing all that enthusiastic, and nothing at all in the area directly around the mill as though it was protected in some way.

Lily heard a high, wavering cry from her left. She looked in that direction, but could see nothing except a flight of birds startled from the trees. The remaining Crules and Curs became immobile for a moment, and then ran off. In an instant, Lily and Sandra were alone.

There was nothing to see but woodland. It was difficult to conceive it was in the middle of a big city, let alone that not long ago the Void of Nothingness had opened here, the Path of Valediction leading the way to another world. She and Sandra might have been out for an early evening amble with their dogs. Dogs. A tear fell, and another. She dashed them away.

"We can get in to the HQ now. Come on," Sandra said, and led the way to the other end of the tumbledown building. Then she disappeared. Lily hurried to the same place and the next minute she was standing upright in a corridor, Sandra next to her apparently unhurt. They walked for a while, down corridors, through doors, eventually arriving in a large room that looked as if it had emptied very suddenly judging by the plates, mugs and cutlery on some of the tables, interrupted card games, papers and pencils, and a few glowing embers still in the fire grate beneath a picture Lily greeting with recognition: 'The Lost World'. Only, it was no longer lost. For some.

People and dogs stumbled in two and three at a time until the room was abuzz with chatter. Lily felt numb. She wondered if that kind of numbness would have stood the test of the Void or if she still didn't know what that really entailed, being an untrained pup and all…

Seb.

A small crystal-flower of ice blossomed within her and eternal winter flowed through her veins.

Sandra finished cleaning and bandaging the last casualty and approached Lily carefully as if afraid she might lash out. Apart from her, and Matt, there was no one else present that Lily recognised.

"Diane?" she queried.

"Gone to the Realm," Sandra said.

"I'm sure she will have made it. She was very good at being unfeeling," Lily said. Sandra looked at her sharply, but Lily maintained an innocent façade.

"My mother?" she said to Sandra. And for the first time she saw Matt's practice nurse exhibit uncertainty. "Where's my mother, Sandra?" Lily hadn't meant her tone to be so curt but anxiety overtook her, fear clutching at her chest.

"She did what she said she would do, Lily. She protected the Realm."

"What do you mean? What happened? Tell me!"

"She went over the edge into the Void and took Credence with her."

Lily sat down hard. She'd been thinking that if Seb wasn't in the Void then neither was Delilah. Just how wrong could she keep being? The floor turned out to be a long way down and she connected with it painfully. She'd only just found her mother, and she'd thrown herself into the Void. Delilah must have had this planned when she'd said goodbye to Lily.

Nothing made any sense any more. She'd been brought up to be unfeeling until she'd left home after a particularly rancid row with Carol. Then she'd not known how to be feeling until she'd been taught it was safe to let her guard down by a big black, hairy Hound who'd bounced into her heart, and she'd learnt to love. Then she'd found a mother she didn't know she had. Lily had hoped to get to know her.

Now she was learning what it was to have that love ripped from her so that she should bleed to death for lack of it.

"She protected the Realm, Lily. She said she would. And she did."

Lily was no longer interested. Bloody Realm! Bloody, bloody Realm! Smacking away the numerous helping hands, she pulled herself upright and left them all there inside their bloody mill headquarters forming their bloody pointless, bloody silly rebellions.

The only way was a guarded way and she was off to get it going. She ignored the cries of her name that followed her through the woods. She kept on walking up the hill until she smelled the traffic congestion, and the pollution produced by too many humans in too small a space. She kept walking, and walking, the pavement making her feet ache. As far as she could see when she got to her house, no one still watched. She was free to go back to her old life.

Lily walked in to her home, locked the door, checked all the windows were secure, closed all the curtains and went to bed. She was never leaving it again. There was no point.

Chapter Twelve

One morning, four months later, Lily dragged herself from her bed and checked the calendar. She'd been avoiding it all this time, but now, yes, it was four months. Why she even bothered looking she didn't know. Seb had said he'd send a gift. She didn't want a gift. She wanted Seb.

What kind of gift could possibly be worth the bother of getting it from the Realm along the Path of Valediction, avoiding the lure of the Void of Nothingness, and then to here? She'd been led to believe that the Path only opened if there were the correct influences at the right time at both ends of it.

Always supposing that's what would happen. But maybe not – maybe Seb had an account with a local florist and he'd pre-ordered delivery of a nice bunch of tulips complete with a little card saying: 'Wish you were here.' Yeah, that would be really great. Not!

Maybe he'd get the local butcher to deliver her a basket of sausages done up in a big bow. She didn't even like sausages. **Food of the Dogs** thundered through her brain and she started to cry. Large, slow tears rolled down her face and dripped unchecked onto her chest. Why couldn't she go more than a few seconds without thinking of him? If only she could blank him out. If only she'd learnt to be properly unfeeling, she'd be so much happier. But he was lodged in her brain. Always there, but never really there.

The front door bell rang. And again. Lily peered through the blind and waited. She waited a long time until, finally, Matt gave up. She could just make out the shape of him, and his dogs, leaving. Sandra would have been ogling his butt. It held no interest for Lily. It might have once upon a time, a lifetime, a world away. A Realm away, even... But not now. She had no interest in consolation.

Even so, Matt came around every day, rang on the doorbell, looked piercingly up at her window, and went away again when she didn't answer. He'd been doing it every day for four months. It was all very well for him to do that but he'd obviously managed to fill any gap left in his life by Caramel Girl's absence. He was always accompanied by at least a couple of dogs, Curs, hybrids, whatever.

Sandra kept Lily informed of Matt's activities as if she were interested. By all accounts, he kept rescuing more and more dogs, he'd got puppy mill farms closed down, he'd caught some unspeakably vile individuals running dog fights; he was going to have to move to a bigger place soon to accommodate all the extra canine company he had these days. He was gaining enemies, too, it would seem, and frequently received hate mail and had his car and house vandalised. Bloody Crules! They were everywhere.

Sandra insisted on getting in every now and then and Lily let her because otherwise she'd be pestered by her father and Carol or other people who thought they had the right 'to keep an eye on her'. Letting Sandra in kept them at bay.

Sandra had tried to get her to go to the doctor for sleeping tablets because Lily couldn't, or wouldn't, sleep. She was afraid to sleep. Every time she lapsed into semi-consciousness she heard Seb in her mind and then she'd wake and then it wouldn't be him. Again. She hated to sleep. By now, the bags under her eyes were damn near down to her knees. They felt like pieces of lead lying on her cheeks. But she refused to get sleeping pills. Sleep was a luxury from a previous life.

Luckily her type of online business meant she could run it entirely from her home. She didn't even have to go to the post office. They came to her and collected all her parcels. It was all she could do to carry on the minimum necessary to keep her business running. She still had bills to pay, after all. Other than that, everything was too much effort and she couldn't be bothered. She spent most of her time trying not to fall asleep.

Dutifully, she went around to her father's place on the last Sunday in the month. Carol still didn't know Lily knew she wasn't really her mother. Lily would pick at the roast dinner presented to her and say, yes she was fine, yes the business was going well, no she wasn't drinking, no she wasn't doing drugs, no, not even clawkle.

There had been no open discussion about the Realm, but it was apparent that they knew all about it. Her father **had** been married to the Great Betrayer's daughter so he must know a lot more than they'd ever let on. As for Carol, Lily thought she must be a Crule-in-training, even if her father wasn't.

Lily and her 'parents' had come to a new understanding with each other. Carol and her father remained of the unfeeling persuasion and spent a lot of time telling Lily that she was now following the right path – she was now behaving more like she should have done all her life. Look what happened when she didn't – she got hurt and that's what happens when you open yourself up and leave yourself unguarded like that. They'd been right all along.

It was better to feel nothing.

Feel nothing, do nothing, be nothing! She could hear Seb say it even though he wasn't actually saying it now.

Oh, shut up! You can't keep nagging me if you can't be bothered being here to do it yourself!

It made her feel worse. She knew she was being unfair. She knew he'd had to go back to the Realm.

She always had to force herself to think of something else. Maybe she should take up some mind-altering substance. It was bound to help. Something must. Her 'parents' appeared concerned that she would start a clawkle habit, guessing there were stacks of it at Credence and Delilah's house. Or rather, Lily's house, according to the documents found stating she was the new owner.

That house was still empty. Lily couldn't decide what to do with it. She didn't feel she could sell it. It belonged, really, to someone active in the Exiles' cause, even though they weren't actually exiles any longer since the Great Reconciliation; they still needed someone to turn to if the need arose. There would always be a need while there were humans to want what wasn't theirs.

She had investigated Delilah's fireplace minutely and was amazed at how difficult it was to see there was an exit at the back of it, as though some kind of illusion had been set to prevent it being seen. Out of curiosity she'd squashed herself through it, bashed her head on the tumble dryer, crept through the lean-to utility room carefully checking there was no one to see her, and dashed into the woods. What now though? She had no idea where to go. She hadn't got to the mill from here the way Delilah had meant her to. Seb had been waiting to throw her on his back and ride off with her into the wind. But not this time. Never again. She spent too long sobbing into the bracken, but she was still abandoned. No matter how many tears she shed Seb didn't come back for her.

Lily had thought she'd have the fireplace bricked up, but she suspected that the exit would still somehow be there even if she did. In the end she merely moved the flower arrangement back in place, inspected it, took out the most moth-eaten elements and replaced them with lots of dried lavender, left the house, and never went back.

So, today was four months from when he'd said he'd send her a gift. It was all a load of hooey though, she knew. He'd been making empty promises to try and make her feel better.

Hooey, hooey? What the bones is hooey? What a great word!

She caught herself on the first snivelling sob and blanked her mind. No more agonising. No more expectations. No more disappointment. She had work to do. After she packed up the orders ready for the mail services man Lily moved to her painting table and got out her most recent efforts. They were hopeless. All the dogs in her pictures looked miserable, as if they'd been treated badly by everyone and their cat. They couldn't be used to produce greeting cards. The only pictures that had any life in them at all, any joy, were the pictures of Seb that she kept painting, seemingly against her will. They just kept coming, all those pictures.

The best seller so far was the one of him bouncing through a field of long grass, ears up, eyes blazing with intelligence, a big grin on his face. In her mind she called it: 'Bouncing through the bullets', but on the back of the card she'd merely called it: 'Joy'.

She was sure the one she was about to finish would outsell 'Joy', though. Lily picked up her brush and carefully placed the highlight in his eye. Seb, upside down, lay back on the sofa, hind legs resting on a footstool, his neck comfortably cushioned, his favourite relaxing position when he felt safe. He had a trilby jammed on his head, dipping down over his face, just one eye showing, and that one opened a squinchy bit to show that nothing got past him. It was at once a picture of complete relaxation and sumptuous bliss. Seb was the most perfect model. He'd known it too. Tears blurred her vision again; rather than risk ruining the painting she put her brush down, went out to the kitchen, and washed up instead.

The doorbell rang and she swore. She could only see who was at the front door from the upstairs window. Hastily she dried her hands and raced along the hall, up the stairs and along the landing to the front of the house, into her bedroom. She peered out of her window. It wasn't that easy to see who was there. Luckily both Matt and Sandra had the habit of ringing the door bell and then standing away from the door a bit and she could easily see it was them. Whoever was there just now had no such consideration and she couldn't see a thing, no matter how hard she tried. Whoever it was must be right up against the front door. Well, there was no way she was going to answer the door unless she first knew who was there.

She made herself comfortable on the windowsill and gazed idly out, waiting to see the caller leave. As she watched, the day darkened, clouds rolled over the sky obscuring the blue, the temperature plummeted and silver streaks of rain slanted across her vision. The doorbell rang again. Whoever was out there would be getting soaked. That wasn't her problem. She stayed right where she was! Then they started banging on the door. The banging got faster. Whoever it was shouldn't be banging on her door. She hadn't asked them to come and bang on her front door. They could sod right off!

But a strange excitement burst into flame and swirled up through her, sparks of light shooting in her head like fireworks into a night sky.

And she couldn't wait any longer. She raced down the stairs two at a time, charged along the hall and threw open the front door.

On the doorstep was a large tuft of hair just like those that Seb had left lying around the place. He reckoned he was sharing his fur lovingly. Her vacuum cleaner hadn't felt loved – it had given up and died after only one cleaning session, long dog hairs well and truly wound around the spindles, clogging up the works.

Lily picked it up. Was this Seb's gift to her? How did he get it here? What was she supposed to do with it? Put it in a locket? What good was that to her? If she'd wanted a lock of his hair all she'd had to do was disembowel her vacuum cleaner!

The rain still fell to the ground, hard enough for the loose gravel edging the path to bounce in the air with its impact.

Lily stood and wondered what was expected of her now.

It was four months since Seb had said he'd send a gift. Was this it, this tuft of hair? Really?

She stepped out into the rain and walked down the path, her slippers unsteady on the wet tiles underfoot. Opening the garden gate she peered out, looking left and right, up and down the road. She pulled back meaning to retreat into the house when the picture in her mind forced itself in front of her eyes. A lone, running figure at the end of the road, galloping along, head up, tail flying. Lily raced back out and checked. Yes, that was what she'd seen. As she watched, it reached the corner at the top of the road.

"Seb!" she screamed. "Seb!" But the figure kept going, not turning, not hesitating. Leaving again.

Had she finally lost it? Was it merely a product of her feverishly overactive imagination? Her hair, which had been completely neglected and allowed to grow too long, was now plastered over her face, rain sticking it to her skin.

Lily looked at the tuft she still held, considerably diminished now by the rain, and knew that she was indeed losing it. The explanation was simple: she hadn't done any cleaning since her Hound had deserted her. This was just another of Seb's tufts, lovingly shared, that had whisked out onto the doorstep in the current of the door opening. That was all. But her fevered and desperate imagination had conjured up a whole scenario that was utterly impossible.

It was highly likely she had imagined the whole thing start to finish. For heaven's sake – talking dogs, people who could cast illusions and make other people kill themselves, strange worlds with silly paths in between them featuring ravenous voids on each side. Maybe she should save everyone the trouble and take herself off to The Haven forthwith. She turned, walked into the house, pushed the door closed behind her and fell on the floor still clutching the tuft, not even sobbing now. Just resigned. Resigned to merely existing, all chance of living gone. Gone with the smell of biscuity fur and sausage-breath.

So when she heard the explosion of breaking glass which she knew signified a missile of some sort bursting through the conservatory window out the back, she didn't care. The sound of the back door splintering was a matter of complete indifference to her. Heavy thuds on the kitchen floor and along the hall approaching her were, apparently, feet. So what?

He told me you might be sulking.

She knew she was hearing things like she'd heard them for the last four months. Things that weren't there.

Yep. My sire was afraid of this. Afraid you'd be sulking. And stubborn enough to keep sulking even when you received his gift.

She clapped her hands over her ears and brought her knees up to her chin.

You can't keep me out.

"You're not really here."

I'm here. Seb's gift to you.

"He left me."

He did what he had to do.

Something grabbed the back of her shirt and yanked her to a sitting position. Amber eyes close to her own, pulled her in to him. Warm breath bathed her face. Oh, how she wanted to believe it this time, but she'd fooled herself too often before.

"You're not real," she murmured.

The broken conservatory window and back door are real. They'll have to be fixed tomorrow.

"You could have come in the front way."

I tried to.

"Not hard enough!"

He told me you were argumentative.

"I'm not argumentative!"

Heck. Heck. And he shook her as if she were a troublesome pup and lay down beside her. Lily slept in Son-of-Seb's furry warmth, her first peaceful sleep for four months.

the end

Also by Susan Alison and available soon…

HOUNDS ABROAD: BOOK TWO
Urban fantasy.

The second book starring Lily, Matt and Hounds.

Staking out the Goat

Romantic comedy sequel to the #1 best-selling 'White Lies and Custard Creams' starring Liz and Moocher.

To receive advance notice of new books you can use the form at the bottom of any of the pages on my website at: www.SusanAlison.com

Glossary

Ageless Chronicles – Ageless Ones keep the memories of everything that happens forever in their joint consciousness – these are the Ageless Chronicles.

Ageless Ones – immortal Hounds who keep the Chronicles. They are made immortal by the judicious use of clawkle.

Ageless Panacea One – an Ageless One able to not only keep the Chronicles, but also foresee some events, and more importantly, work out what they mean.

Betrayed (the) – the Realm, ie Hounds and Compeers

Casting Out – the Hounds, after the Great Betrayer Wars, threw all the Compeers out of the Realm in the Casting Out.

Clawkle – a plant that grows in the Realm from the roots of which mind-altering substances are produced.

Clawk-head – a clawkle addict.

Compeer – a comrade, companion, close friend, one part of a symbiotic relationship.

Crule – a human gone bad. They are everywhere. They have no compassion, no feeling for others, no interests except their own. Crules have been around for as long as humans have – anywhere someone is suffering, a Crule will be sipping their tears of agony, mental or physical. They cannot be killed, only imprisoned.

Crules-in-training – are everywhere. They start by being unkind. They're quick learners.
Curs –dogs that have been taught by Crules to go over to the dark side. They can easily be brought back with kindness.

Exiles – Compeers and their descendants after they were cast out of the Realm.

Fangry – Seb's teeth, or anyone's teeth that are big, white, well-looked after, but most importantly – scary!

Great Betrayer (the) – she who brought the Crule to the Realm as her mate, from which stemmed the Great Betrayer Wars and the Casting Out of the Compeers.

Haven (the) – thought of locally as a hospital, influential Crules use it to imprison any Compeers and their descendants that they can identify.

Heck, heck – Seb's laugh, with which he was always generous.

Human Territories – the Earth, the human world.

Leepig – long-legged, furry creatures who live to be chased by Hounds. They love it, and are always approaching the Hounds' dens and yowling for a good chase game.

Path of Valediction – leads the way to the Realm and other worlds. The Void of Nothingness is always on either side of it, waiting for the unwary. The Path appears in response to the right person being at both ends of it. It has to be someone who can do it, like Caramel Girl or an Ageless One or a full-blown Crule, like Credence.

Realm (the) – the world from which Seb and Caramel Girl have come in an attempt to save it by enabling reconciliation with their Compeers.

Sebastian Hounds – the guardians of the Realm.

The One Who Knows… – Lily

Made in the USA
Charleston, SC
18 August 2015